C. Hare Augustus J.

Days in Rome

C. Hare Augustus J.

Days in Rome

ISBN/EAN: 9783337380731

Printed in Europe, USA, Canada, Australia, Japan

Cover: Foto ©Andreas Hilbeck / pixelio.de

More available books at **www.hansebooks.com**

MANUAL OF EDUCATION:

A

BRIEF HISTORY

OF THE

Rhode Island Institute of Instruction,

INCLUDING

A SYNOPSIS OF ANNUAL AND OTHER MEETINGS,

LIST OF OFFICERS AND MEMBERS,

TOGETHER WITH

THE CONSTITUTION AND CHARTER,

BY

EDWIN MARTIN STONE.

PROVIDENCE:
PROVIDENCE PRESS COMPANY, PRINTERS.
1874.

PREFACE.

The following pages have been written at the request of the *Rhode Island Institute of Instruction*, expressed by vote of its members at the annual meeting in 1871. The publication has been delayed beyond the time originally contemplated, by circumstances not under the author's control. In preparing this volume it has been the aim to present a comprehensive view of the state of education in Rhode Island in the early years of its history, and to trace the progressive steps by which the cause has advanced to its present cheering condition. The founding of the INSTITUTE, under the auspices of far-seeing and guiding minds, was an event the importance of which cannot be over-estimated. It was the embodying of hitherto scattered elements, and imparting to them a power which separately they did not possess. In educating the Public Mind so that it should perceive and feel the duty which society owes to the rising generation; in securing to teaching as a profession, a higher appreciation; in developing just ideas of the relation between intellectual culture and prosperous industry; in awakening a worthy ambition to make the Public Schools the most efficient auxiliaries to the higher institutions of learning; and in demanding that all which science reveals, experience approves, and moral principle enforces, shall be made subsidiary to popular education; the INSTITUTE has borne a part upon which its members may look with entire satisfaction. And if there be truth in the often-quoted proverb, "coming events cast their shadows before," there is foundation for the belief that the future glory of its work will far surpass the brightness of its past.

To the Teachers and Friends of Education in Rhode Island this "Brief History" is respectfully inscribed, with the hope that it may prove an acceptable contribution to a Cause which is now engaging so earnestly their hearts and hands.

E. M. S.

November, 1874.

HISTORY.

PRELIMINARY to the history of the RHODE ISLAND INSTI-
TUTE OF INSTRUCTION, it will be proper to glance at the
condition of Education in the early days of the Colony
of Rhode Island, and the rise and progress of her Public
School System.

If the Cause of Public Education in Rhode Island, now so
universally popular, did not at an early day engage the attention of the Body Politic here, as in other Colonies, the
neglect, seeming or real, should be attributed rather to the
peculiar circumstances under which this Colony was settled
than to a want of appreciation of good learning. It will be
borne in mind when making a contrast between the early
educational condition of Rhode Island and that of her
neighbor Colonies, that she labored under difficulties which
constituted no part of their experience; and that while the
settlements at Plymouth, Boston, Salem and New Haven,
were begun with organized bodies of men, bringing with
them means for at once establishing the Church and the School
House, our Colony Life was begun by a handful of Refugees
from their first chosen home in the Bay Colony, too few in
numbers to do more at the outstart than to subdue enough of
the wilderness to make for themselves an unenviable home;
too poor to command at the moment and put in operation the
agencies of a high civilization; and too much occupied in
protecting themselves against aboriginal and other dangers to
establish, as a first step, the Public School and the University.

Had they been differently situated, a different aspect would
doubtless have been put upon the face of things in these
Plantations. The Leader of the Conscience Band who fled
first to Seekonk, and then, at the suggestion of the friendly
Winslow, and possibly of the no less friendly Winthrop, removed to a spot he named Providence,—was a profound
scholar, and could not but have had a just comprehension of
the importance of a practical education to a rising community. But the children of the Plantation Colony, for several
years after its founders arrived here, must have been so few
as hardly to have suggested the immediate necessity of a
school,*while the pressing demands upon the time and services
of Williams in adjusting local vexations and in serving the
welfare of a neighboring Colony, put it out of his power to
give thought to any plan for establishing a system of popular
education. Yet it is not to be assumed that no interest was
felt here or elsewhere in the Colony on this subject, or that
no measures were adopted for the encouragement of education. In 1640, one year after the settlement of Newport was
begun, that town invited Mr. Robert Lenthal "to keep a
public school for the learning of youth, and for his encouragement there was granted to him and his heirs one hundred
acres of land, and four more for a house lot." The town
also voted, " that one hundred acres should be laid forth and
appropriated for a school, for the encouragement of the poorer
sort, to train up their youth in learning."†

These one hundred acres, it is supposed by some, were
originally located in what is now the town of Middletown,
and in 1661 were exchanged for a tract subsequently known as
Newtown, or school land. In 1663, this trust was ordered to

* It should be borne in mind that in 1680 the population of Rhode Island, exclusive of Indians, did not exceed 7,000, and in 1701, sixty-five years after the settlement of Providence, it had increased to only 10,000. Of this population, the largest
portion must have been comprised in the settlements at Providence, Newport
and Warwick. In other parts of the Colony the necessity for schools could not
have been pressing.

† Arnold, i. 145, 146.

be divided into lots, "and to be sold or loaned on condition that the purchasers should pay to the town treasurer an annual rent to constitute a fund for the schooling and educating of poor children, according to the direction of the town council for the time being."* From 1775 to 1792 there were seventy-eight lots in Newtown, denominated "school lands," for which the town received in rents, $181.42 per annum.

In 1695, Judge Samuel Sewall, of Boston, conveyed land in the Pettaquamscut Purchase to Trustees, the income of which was to be appropriated to the support of the ministry, and to the instruction of "the children and youths of the above mentioned town of Pettaquamscut,† as well English there settled, or to be settled, as Indians the aboriginal natives and proprietors of the place, to read and write the English language and the rules of grammar." The school was for a long time at Tower Hill, and among the instructors were Constant Southworth, Increase Hewett, and Robert F. Noyes.‡

In the following year (1696) Judge Sewall conveyed to Harvard College land in the same Purchase " for and towards the support and education at said College, of such youths whose parents may not be of sufficient ability to maintain them there, especially such as shall be sent from Pettaquamscut aforesaid, English or Indians."§ In 1765, Thomas Ninigret, commonly known as King Tom, Sachem of the Narragansetts, petitioned the Society for Propagating the Gospel to establish a Free School for the children of the tribe. Ninigret was born in 1736, and became Sachem in 1746.

In 1697, Newport voted other school lands for the benefit of a school master. In 1706, a school house was built at the public charge. To defray the expense the town sold six acres of land, and laid a tax of £150. In 1713, the town voted to establish another school, and Benjamin Nicholson was chosen schoolmaster.‖ In 1726, one hundred and six acres of land

* Barnard's Report, 1848, p. 115,

† Now Exeter.

‡ Potter's Early History of Narragansett, pp. 290, 291.   § Ibid.

‖ In 1716, Portsmouth "having considered how excellent an ornament learning

were voted for a school house in the eastern part of the town. From this date until the American Revolution, a commendable interest in the cause of education was manifested in Newport – an interest that for a time was paralyzed by the influences of the war.   In 1795 the Long Wharf Association of Newport, adopted measures to establish a public school, and provided for its support.   The same year Mr. Simeon Potter, of Swansea, Mass., gave to the Association, in trust, an estate in that town, "to support a Free School forever."

In 1827, a public school system in a modified form, was carried into effect, and in 1828, Governor Fenner contributed $100 to the school fund of Newport, "instead of giving the time honored 'treat' to the people on election day,"—the usual expense of the treat being that amount.   From this period, the interest in popular education has advanced in that city, and at the present time the public schools there are among the best in the State.

Providence, in 1663, laid out and reserved "one hundred acres of upland land and six acres of meadow (or lowland to the quantity of eight acres, in lieu of meadow,") "for the maintenance of a school."   Previous to this, home instruction or a Dame's school, probably, answered the needs of the children of the town.

The first recorded acts of the citizens of Bristol in relation to schools bears date September, 1682, when it was voted, "that each person that hath children in town ready to go to school, shall pay three pence the week for each child's schooling to the schoolmaster, and the town by rate according to each ratable estate shall make the wages to amount to £24 the year.   The selectmen to look out a grammar schoolmaster and use their endeavor to obtain £5 of the cape money granted for such an end."   "September, 1648, voted £24 the

is to mankind," adopted measures to build a school house on the south side of the town.   Six years later two other school houses were built.—Arnold's R. I., ii., 59.

year for Mr. Cobbett, he officiating in the place of a school-master in this town."*

From an early date Bristol has been fortunate in its choice of committees, whose labors have been effective in giving a high character to the schools of that town.

Although "no public education at the expense of the town" was provided for in Warren, previous to 1828, the public records of Swansea, Mass., of which Warren was a part until 1718, show that becoming care was taken to secure for its children and youth the benefit of educational instruction. The same is true of Barrington, also a part of Swansea, and which was erected into a distinct township in 1717. As early as 1673, " three years after old Plymouth had voted a freeschool within her borders,"† a school was set up "for the teaching of grammar, rhetoric, and arithmetic, and the tongues of Latin, Greek and Hebrew, also to read English and to write." Of this school Rev. John Myles was appointed master, at "at a salary of £40 per annum in current country pay." Whether or not this sum was intended as a full equivalent for his services as clergyman and school teacher, there seems, at a later day, to have been differences of opinion. In 1699, Mr. Jonathan Bosworth was appointed "to teach in the several places in the town by course," at a compensation of £18 per year, "one-quarter in money and the other three-quarters in provisions, at money price." In 1702, Mr. John Devotion was chosen to fulfil similar peripatetic duties at a salary of " £12 current money of New England, to be paid quarterly, and the town to ' pay for his diet,' " besides an allowance of 20s. " towards the keeping of his horse."‡

From 1718 until 1828, when regular appropriations of money for public education by the town first begun to be

---

* These facts have been cited to show that from a very early date the education of the young was not undervalued, nor wholly unprovided for.

† Bicknell's History Barrington, p. 91.

‡ Fessenden's History Warren, pp. 83, 84.

made, the people of Warren have not been unmindful of the
intellectual needs of the young, and the steady advance of
public sentiment has secured to that town school convenien-
cies and advantages that will compare favorably with those of
other communities.

The public school idea, now developed into grand propor-
tions which renders it the glory of the State, was slow of
growth. Like some of the beautiful productions of nature,
its bloom and fruitage could not be prematurely forced. It
found, however, through a long series of years, faithful culti-
vators, who, amidst the temporary expedients of private
schools and of proprietors' schools, persevered in watching
over and protecting the precious plant, resting in hope of its
ultimate perfection. Among the most conspicuous of these,
dating from 1684, when William Turpin was the first schoolmaster in Providence of whom any memorial remains,* until
1799, were John Dexter, William Hopkins, Joseph Whipple,

* It would be interesting to learn something more than is now known of the experience of Mr. Turpin as a teacher. His native place and the year of his arrival
in Providence, is unknown. The earliest record of him found bears date June
11th, 1684, on which day he covenanted with William Hawkins and his wife Lydia,
" to furnish Peregrine Gardner with board and schooling one year for six pounds;
forty shillings of which in beef and pork; pork at two-pence, and beef at three-
pence half-penny, per lb.; twenty shillings in corn, at two shillings per bushel;
and the balance in silver money."–(Staples's Annals.) That Mr. Turpin intended
to make teaching a permanent occupation in Providence, is evident from the fact
that in January, 1685, he petitioned the town to invest him and his heirs with the
land set apart " for the use and benefit of a school master," " so long as he or any
of them should maintain that worthy art of teaching."– (Town Records.) That
his petition was granted the records do not show. Mr. Turpin must have been
held in universal respect, and have possessed the confidence of his fellow-towns-
men as a man of discreet judgment and unimpeachable integrity, as we find that
he twice represented Providence in the General Assembly, was one year Town
Clerk, and for upwards of fourteen years was Town Treasurer. He died in the
early part of 1744. His house stood on the west side of North Main street, nearly
opposite the fourth Baptist meeting house. At one time the General Assembly
held their sessions there. According to a statement made by the late Mr. Samuel
Thurber, " this was a very sightly place, and a place of considerable business.
He had a large yard with an elm tree in it, a fine garden, handsomely fenced in,
through which there ran a small brook, which came from a swamp laying a little
to the eastward of where the meeting house now is."

Nicholas Cooke, Joseph Olney, Esek Hopkins, Elisha Brown, John Mawney, Nicholas Brown, Elijah Tillinghast, Daniel Abbot, Barzillai Richmond, John Brown, John Jenckes, Nathaniel Greene, Charles Keene, Darius Sessions, Samuel Nightingale, Jabez Bowen, Moses Brown, Enos Hitchcock, James Manning, Theodore Foster, William Jones, Richard Jackson, John Howland, Samuel Thurber, Grindall Reynolds, Nathan Fisher, Peter Grinnell, Jonathan Maxcy, Joseph Jenckes, James Burrill, Jr., David L. Barnes, George R. Burrill, Samuel W. Bridgham, Stephen Gano, John Carlisle, Thomas P. Ives, Joel Metcalf, Richard Anthony, and William Richmond.

In 1767, an important advance step was taken in Providence in the direction of "providing schools for all the children of the inhabitants." Hon. Jabez Bowen wrote a report which was laid before a town meeting, January 1, 1768, embracing a system of public instruction. In this it was provided :

"That every inhabitant of this town, whether they be free of the town or not, shall have and enjoy an equal right and privilege, of sending their own children and the children of others that may be under their care, for instruction and bringing up to any or all of said schools."

But the time for a full appreciation of this recommendation had not arrived, and it was rejected. In 1791, President Manning, of Brown University, as chairman of a committee to whom a petition of some citizens for the establishment of public schools had been referred, drew up a report recommending substantially what Gov. Bowen had proposed twenty-four years before. This report was presented at a town meeting, held August 1, and accepted, though it contained an obnoxious clause which prevented any further action being taken upon it.*

* This clause recommended that as the Friends then had a school of their own in which their children were instructed and would continue to be instructed, they should be permitted to draw from the town treasury money to support their school in proportion to the number of children attending it.

Thus far the action of Providence had been local in its character, viz. : to establish free schools within its own limits. In 1798, a new era dawned upon the State. A movement was commenced in Providence to expand the public school idea, and accomplish for every town in Rhode Island what had thus far been attempted in her principal capital. In other words to establish, by legislative enactment, a *State Public School System*. A leading man in this enterprise was John Howland, who found himself ably sustained by earnest men of various professions and occupations. Mr. Howland was distinguished for sound judgment, far-reaching discernment, skill in execution, and unconquerable persistence. His position in the community gave him a strong influence with the wealthy and with the laboring classes, and as the hostility to free schools was found largely among the latter, he was able to do much to create a better sentiment among them. In his place of business, in the street, and by the fire-side, free public schools was made by him a topic of conversation. He agitated the subject in town meeting, and in the Mechanics' Association, then the most influential organization in Providence. Under the direction of that Association, and in its name, he wrote a memorial which was presented to the General Assembly at its February session in East Greenwich, in 1799, soliciting that honorable body " to make legal provision for the establishment of free schools, sufficient to educate all the children in the several towns throughout the State."* The memorial was referred to a Committee, which reported by bill at the June session the same year. The bill was printed, and referred to the freemen for instruction. The instructions given by the town of Providence to its representatives to vote for the bill, were written by Mr. Howland. They set forth that "on the question of free schools all party distinctions are broken down. Here there can be no clashing

* The Representatives from Providence at this session of the General Assembly were John Smith, Thomas P. Ives and David L. Barnes, all of whom were steadfast friends of public free schools.

of interests. On this subject one section of the State cannot
be opposed to another. Before this benevolent idea, every
partial, narrow motive of local policy must disappear."* At
the October session of the General Assembly the bill was
passed by the House of Representatives, but in the Senate it
was postponed until the session in February, 1800, when that
body concurred with the House, and a public free school law
became an established fact. This law continued in force
three years, when it was repealed. But in that three years
the tree of knowledge, thus legally planted, had struck deep
and spread wide its roots, and exhibited a vitality that bid
defiance to the destructive influence of mal-legislation."†

It seems surprising, at this late day, that a system for the
free education of all classes, should have been so soon abro-
gated. Yet, it is no more surprising than that, in 1818, a

---

* It is worthy of record here that the repeal of the school law had no injurious
effect upon the schools in Providence, but rather stimulated their friends to more
earnest endeavors in their behalf. The system was continued unchanged, except
by such improvements as time and experience suggested. From year to year
they increased in usefulness and in favor with the people. The firm position
taken by the friends of education in that town, and the success to which the
school system there voluntarily maintained, attained, attracted attention in every
part of the state, and did much to rally public sentiment by which the passage of
the school law of 1828 was secured. In the subsequent efforts from that date to
1850 made to carry forward the work of education so as to meet the demands of
an increasing intelligence, the disinterested services of Francis Wayland, Samuel
W. Bridgham, Alexis Caswell, Alexander Duncan, John L. Hughes, William T.
Grinnell, William S. Patten, Esek Aldrich, S. Augustus Arnold, J. P. K. Henshaw,
Seth Padelford, George Baker, William Gammell, Moses B. Ives, Thomas M. Burgess, Edward R. Young, and the members of the School Committee generally,
were invaluable. Since 1850, the same spirit has prevailed, and it is safe to say
that the schools of Providence, in their several grades, are not elsewhere surpassed. The High School takes rank with the best in the country.

† The rise and progress of the public schools in Providence forms one of the most
interesting chapters in the history of Education in Rhode Island. Those who wish
to learn more of its details than are here given may consult the Life of John Howland, and Barnard's "Report and Documents relating to the Public Schools of
Rhode Island." In all his efforts in behalf of popular education Mr. Howland was
encouraged by the support of Rev. Drs. Hitchcock, Maxcy, and Gano, Governor
William Jones, Richard Jackson, Jabez Bowen, James Burrill, Jr., Amos M. At-
well, and other influential citizens of the town.

proposition to establish primary schools in Boston, should have been opposed, or than the indifference to educational improvement that prevailed with the people of Massachusetts as late as 1840. In a lecture delivered at Topsfield, in that State, before the Essex County Teachers' Association, by the late Horace Mann, then Secretary of the Board of Education, he said: "In our own times, in such low estimation is this highest of all causes held, that in these days of conventions for all other objects of public interest,—when men go hundreds of miles to attend railroad conventions, and cotton conventions, and tobacco conventions, and when the delegates of political conventions are sometimes counted, as Xerxes counted his army, by acres and square miles,—yet such has often been the dispersive effect upon the public of announcing a common school convention, and a lecture on education, that I have queried in my own mind whether, in regard to two or three counties, at least, in our own State, it would not be advisable to alter the law for quelling riots and mobs; and, instead of summoning sheriffs and armed magistrates and the *posse comitatus* for their dispersion, to put them to flight by making proclamation of a discourse on common schools." But this sharp sarcasm of Mr. Mann had a wider application than he gave it. At the time it was uttered a general apathy prevailed among the people of the New England States, as it did among those of all the other States in the Union, in regard to the condition of public free school education,—an apathy that required the utmost efforts of earnest workers to remove.

In 1844, more than seven thousand school houses in the State of New York were destitute of suitable play grounds, while nearly six thousand were unprovided with convenient seats and desks, and in almost every other respect were unfit for the uses for which they were erected.*

---

* The State Commissioner says, "nearly eight thousand were destitute of the proper facilities for ventilation, and upwards of six thousand without a privy of any sort, while of the remainder but about one thousand [out of nine thousand three hundred and sixty-eight] were provided with privies containing different apartments for male and female pupils!"

In 1847, a depreciation in the effectiveness of the schools in many parts of Pennsylvania was reported. In New Jersey it was declared that, to establish a Normal School, " would be an infringement of the rightful liberty of the citizen," while of Indiana it was said by one of her own sons, " We have *borrowed* millions for the physical improvement of our State, but we have not *raised* a dollar by advalorem taxation to cultivate the minds of our children ! " *

These citations are not made for the purpose of covering the deficiencies of Rhode Island by pointing out the defects of sister States, but merely to show that an almost criminal indifference to the education of the masses was universal, and that the need of reformation in our own State was but a sample of needs felt and acknowledged throughout the country.

In 1843, public sentiment had so far advanced in the right direction, that Governor Fenner was authorized by the General Assembly to appoint a State Agent, whose duty it should be to use all legitimate means for promoting the interests of education in every town in Rhode Island, and thus aid in awakening a new enthusiasm, and in raising to a higher level the standard of instruction. In the same year, Hon. Henry Barnard, of Connecticut, was appointed to fill this office, upon the duties of which he entered with characteristic zeal. His time was constantly employed in visiting the different towns in the State, delivering lectures, holding educational meetings, editing an educational journal, establishing free libraries, and in other ways doing an almost incredible amount of work.

During a lapse of nearly twenty-eight years, the great mistake of the General Assembly of 1803, in repealing the school law, was painfully apparent all over the State. Every town had thereby been left to do what seemed right in its own eyes—to make provision for schools or not—and in all towns in which the popular mind had not been enlightened

* Address to the Legislature of Indiana, by one of the people, 1847.

by the inculcation of generous views, and stimulated to action by a strong sense of public duty, the means of education were lamentably deficient. Under this state of things, "Proprietors Schools" took form, with a view of securing for the young the education they were otherwise in danger of losing. The proprietors school houses were built and owned by a company of individuals who employed a teacher at their own expense to educate their children. Others, not proprietors, but having children, were permitted to send them to the same schools, by paying a fixed sum for tuition. To both classes, therefore, these were "pay schools." But this arrangement, though conferring a benefit upon many who otherwise would have become outcasts from the commonwealth of letters, failed to answer the growing wants of the State. In 1827, the friends of a wiser policy made a grand effort for a change. That year, at the October session of the General Assembly, a memorial was presented, asking for the establishing of "a general system of education, extended at the public expense, to all the citizens of the State." On the basis of that memorial, plans for organizing a system of free schools was brought before the General Assembly, by John B. Waterman, of Warwick, Joseph L. Tillinghast, of Providence, and others, which were embodied in "An Act to establish Public Schools," and ably advocated at the January session, 1828, by Messrs. Waterman, Tillinghast, Dixon, of Westerly, and Potter, of South Kingstown. After a protracted discussion, the bill passed the house by a vote of fifty-seven in the affirmative and two in the negative. It passed the Senate, with a few amendments, without a dissenting voice. The amendments were concurred in by the House, and the foundation was thus a second time laid for a Public School System in Rhode Island.

The law underwent various changes and modifications until 1844, when the "Agent of Public Schools" was directed to prepare the draft of a school law, in which the various public and special acts on the subject should be consolidated, and such additional provisions engrafted as should be thought necessary or desirable. This was done by Mr. Barnard with great completeness.

To this Act, the late Hon. Wilkins Updike, then a member of the House of Representatives, gave an earnest and powerful support. In a highly effective speech, setting forth " the wide-spread disaffection with the schools as they are," and " the inefficient manner in which the system is administered," the dilapidated condition of school houses, the need of better qualified teachers, and the duty of the State and of the towns to do more than had been done for the support of schools, he added : " We must elect capable men to the office of school committees, and men of education and wealth must consent to act as committees. These committees must see that none but moral and qualified teachers are employed, and that our young men and young women may qualify themselves to be teachers, let us contribute of our means as individuals to establish and maintain model schools and Normal schools. Let us have our RHODE ISLAND INSTITUTE OF INSTRUCTION, which shall meet in different parts of the State, where teachers and the friends of education may come together and discuss the great subject which concerns the improvement of the public schools. Let us go round into districts and point out to parents and to our fellow-citizens generally, existing defects, and all desirable and practical remedies, in the management and government of these schools."

" But let us start right. Let us have an organization to begin with, so that our efforts will not be thrown away, and our money squandered as now. Let us have a law by which good schools can be established if we can convince the people that it is their interest to establish them. Let us have a law by which none but qualified teachers shall be employed. . . . . Let us have a law by which the enormous evil and expense arising out of a constant change of school books shall be remedied : and all new school houses erected after judicious plans and directions. . . . . Let us have an

3

officer whose intelligence, experience, and constant oversight shall give efficiency and uniformity to the administration of the system—who shall go round among the schools, hold meetings of teachers, parents and the friends of education, break up the apathy which prevails in some parts of the State, enlighten the ignorant, and direct the efforts of all to one great and glorious end, the training of all the children, the rich and the poor, in all sound and worthy practice. Let us have a State pride on this subject. Let us aim to be, what I am sure we can become, from our compact population, and the comparative wealth of all our people, the educated and educating State of this Union. . . . . Let the census of the United States, and above all, let peace in our own borders, the security of property, the dignity and value of labor, the cheerfulness and happiness of every fireside and workshop in the State, proclaim, that there is not a child of suitable age, who is not at school, or an inhabitant of the State who cannot read or write, or who has not access to a well-selected library of good books."

State Commissioner.

The Act thus advocated, was passed at the June session of the General Assembly, 1844, to take effect in July, 1845. By this Act, the office of Commissioner of Public Schools was established, and with extended powers took the place of the State agency.

Mr. Barnard had not been long engaged in a survey of the State by which he was made familiar with the local hindrances to the progress of his work, before he became sensible of the need of an organization, embracing alike practical educators and the friends of education, through which the people could be more frequently reached than it would be possible for him alone to do, and which at the same time by its moral support would impart increased efficiency to his own endeavors. Out of this need came the RHODE ISLAND INSTITUTE OF INSTRUCTION, whose history, in these pages, is briefly recorded.

Formation of the Institute.

In the latter part of the year 1844, at the suggestion of Mr. Barnard, Mr. Amos Perry, then Principal of the Summer Street Grammar School, in Providence, made arrangements for a meeting of teachers and the friends of education to be held in the City Council chamber, to consider the subject of organizing an association, whose object should be to awaken among the people a broader and deeper interest in public schools, and at the same time lend its support to Mr. Barnard in his work as State Commissioner. The meeting was held according to previous notice, at which Nathan Bishop, Esq., Superintendent of Public Schools in Providence, presided. Twenty-five or thirty teachers, most of them engaged in the public schools, and a few other persons were present. Mr. Barnard being unable to attend in consequence of severe indisposition, Mr. Perry explained the object of the meeting, stating, in substance, Mr. Barnard's views and wishes. After a free interchange of opinions, during which several gentlemen manifested a want of faith in associate action, a committee was appointed to consider the expediency of forming a State Educational Association, and to take such measures for that object as they should deem expedient. This committee consisted of John Kingsbury, Nathan Bishop, Amos Perry, Henry Day, and John J. Stimson.

The representative character of the committee will be noted. All of them were identified with the cause of education. One member was at the head of a private school; one Superintendent of the Public Schools; one at the head of a Grammar school; one the senior teacher in the High school, and one an influential member of the School Committee. The several meetings of this committee were held in the office of the Superintendent of Public Schools. After deliberately considering the question, shall we have an Association? it was agreed that the enterprise should go forward, and the foundation of the Institute was laid. "Thenceforward," says one actively engaged in the preliminary movement, "there was no discussion about the importance of combined or associate action. It became a necessity. Obstacles and obstructions of whatever nature gradually disappeared. The officers were selected, after a careful canvass, with a view to their qualifications and usefulness. Friends whom we had never known came forward and lent a helping hand. After a year or two instead of witnessing the decline and death that had been foretold, we had from the same lips a more hopeful prediction. This time the INSTITUTE was to live and prosper a hundred years. This sentiment uttered in a strain of eloquence in the First Baptist meeting-house was received with applause by attentive listeners, and influences were thrown in favor of such broad and manly action as tends to such a result.

"The Association adopted the name of the eldest educational association of the country, with a view of indicating, on a restricted scale, its general policy and mode of action. The two associations were alike in their general outlines, though different in their sphere of action. One belonged to New England, or the nation, and the other to the little State of Rhode Island. While teachers naturally took a leading part in the deliberations of the Institute, all friends of education without regard to profession or calling, were invited to co-operate for the common cause and to share the honors and responsibilities of membership. Exclusiveness and clannishness were foreign to its spirit and object. A free and cordial intercourse between different classes and professions was invited and encouraged, with a view to breaking down partition walls and introducing life and light to the dark chambers of the mind. It was remarked by Mr. Barnard when the plan of organization was under consideration, that education is many-sided and is best promoted by a combination of influences from various sources." *

* Letter from Hon. Amos Perry to the author.

To the foregoing account a few particulars may be added. The adjourned meeting referred to was held in the State House in Providence, January 21, 1845, when the committee to whom the whole subject had been committed, made a report which is here presented, as expressing the feelings and convictions of those earliest in the movement :

" Whatever doubt may exist in regard to the influences of popular education, in other countries, there can be none in regard to the United States. *Here*, it *may* be assumed as an axiom. that the people, the *whole* people should be educated. Our institutions, civil, political, and religious, all imperatively demand it. *How* shall this be done? is the only question that admits of discussion. To this question only one rational answer can be given—chiefly by public or common schools.

" Whatever influence may be exerted by the press, by the college, and high schools, in advancing education,—and we have no doubt but *that* influence is great and indispensable; it is not for a moment to be supposed that these means are sufficient to educate a *whole people.* History does not present a solitary example of a country or province, where education has been universal, without some instrumentality analogous to common schools.

" Literature and science may flourish where only the *wealthy few* are highly educated. It is possible that the *few*, by monopolizing the emoluments and privileges which superior knowledge confers, may, while the many are toiling in agriculture or mechanic arts, rise to higher attainments, and cause science and literature to take deeper root and to bring forth mature fruits. Though such fruits might bring blessings with them, the genius of our institutions requires rather the diffusion than the accumulation of knowledge. It was the boast of Henry IV , of France, that he would ' take care that every peasant should be in such a condition as to have a fowl in his pot.' It should be the care of *our country* that *every child should be educated.*

" Our forefathers laid us under deep obligation, therefore, when they consecrated the common school to the education of the people. Ought we not deeply to regret that within our own State, that mission has not been fully accomplished. There are those among us who cannot read or write. Never should the friends of education rest till this stain is wiped from the escutcheon of the State. Though we hail with delight the deep interest now beginning to be awakened in different parts of the State, still it is an important question, what further can be done to give our public school system an impulse so vigorous, as to send its full st blessings to the most secluded district.

Light must be diffused in regard to the subject. Parents must be roused from apathy by having the evils of ignorance and the blessings of knowledge placed before them; the connection between crime and ignorance

must be shown; it must be demonstrated that knowledge not only leads to
higher elevation of character here, and better hopes of a future life, but
it must be proved that an intelligent, educated man will earn more
money than an ignorant one; the incompetency of teachers must be ex-
posed, and public sentiment must be made to demand better; in short,
we should all be brought to the full conviction that good public schools
are a powerful safeguard of our country. In view of these and similar
considerations, we deem it expedient to form, at the present time, a State
Association for the promotion of public school education."

This report, after being discussed, was referred to a committee of which Mr. Barnard was chairman, with instructions
to present a constitution at an adjourned meeting. This
meeting at which Hon. Wilkins Updike, of South Kingstown,
presided, was held in Westminster Hall on the evening of
January 25, 1845, when the constitution, prepared by Mr.
Barnard, was reported and adopted. At an adjourned meeting held in the Vestry of the First Baptist Church, on the
28th of January, the organization of the INSTITUTE was completed by the choice of the following officers : •

President, - - -	JOHN KINGSBURY, Providence.
Vice Presidents, - - -	WILKINS UPDIKE, South Kingstown.
	ARIEL BALLOU, Woonsocket.
Corresponding Secretary, - -	NATHAN BISHOP, Providence.
Recording Secretary, - -	JOSHUA D. GIDDINGS, Providence.
Treasurer, - - - -	THOS. C. HARTSHORN, Providence.
Directors, - - -	WILLIAM GAMMELL, Providence,
	AMOS PERRY, Providence,
	CALEB FARNUM, Providence,
	JOSEPH T SISSON, North Providence,
	J. T. HARKNESS, Smithfield,
	J. B. TALLMAN, Cumberland,
	L. W. BALLOU, Cumberland,
	J. S. TOURTELLOTT, Glocester.
	SAMUEL GREENE, Smithfield.

During the first year of the Institute, spirited meetings
under its auspices were held in Providence, Newport, Bristol,
Warren, Woonsocket, East Greenwich, Valley Falls, Chepachet, Olneyville, Scituate, Fruit Hill, Pawtuxet, Foster,

and Kingston. At these meetings the following topics were discussed :

" How parents can coöperate with teachers."

" The value of a sound public opinion on the subject of education."

" That the whole community, and not a part, should be educated."

" Methods of disciplining and managing schools."

"The necessity of a graduation of schools."

" Methods of securing good teachers."

" Public schools the only available method of educating the entire community."

" Importance of educating the young morally as well as intellectually."

" Methods of teaching reading."

" Methods of teaching spelling."

" Music as a branch of education in schools."

" That a State, in order to make the most of its resources, must know how to use them."

" That a State will increase in wealth in proportion to the intelligence of its population."

The programme of the Teachers' Institute held in 1847, under the general supervision of the State Commissioner, indicates the practical character of those meetings, and is a fair sample of the work engaged in during the earlier years of struggle for a higher educational life. It is as follows :

" 1. A review of the studies usually taught in the public schools of this State, with exemplifications of the best method of instruction in each branch, and with special attention to such difficulties as any member of the Institute may have encountered in teaching the same.

" 2. Familiar lectures and discussions among the members, on the organization of schools, the classification of pupils, and the theory and practice of teaching.

" Public lectures and discussions in the evening, on topics calculated to interest parents and the community generally. in the subject of education, and the organization, administration. and improvement of schools."

Every teacher was requested to communicate a list of such topics as he wished to have considered at the session of the Institute which he proposed to attend,—to be provided with.

a Bible or Testament, a slate and pencil, with pen and ink or lead pencil, and a blank or common-place book in which to enter notes, and also with the reading book used by the first class in the town where he taught, or proposed to teach. By this method the meetings of the Institute became, in large degree, mutual improvement seasons.

The topics presented and discussed brought out the best thoughts of practical teachers. Their mutual experiences in the school district and in the school-room, related in a free and unstudied conversation, became a valuable treasure to each; and as they returned to their daily duties, they felt that they had not only been refreshed by the social enjoyments of these occasions, but had found new helps to future success in their vocation.

At the first annual meeting, held in Providence, January 15, 1846, the President, in a brief review of the year, said:

"Through this Association, and county societies of a similar nature, a vast amount of voluntary labor, in this cause, has been performed; and, apparently, a very deep public interest has been created. By these means, united with legislative action, a train of measures has been put in motion which already indicate a great improvement in the public mind—a train, which, if not prematurely interrupted, will ultimately, and at no distant period, raise the public schools of this State to the highest rank among the means of popular education. It is not too much to say, that probably no State in the Union has made greater progress in the same space of time. . . . . . I venture to predict that if the friends of education, as they have hitherto done, shun all partizan and sectarian alliances, those who choose to throw themselves as impediments in the way of this cause, will wage a war which will recoil upon their own heads. Let us, then, go forward with steady courage and cheerful hearts. Let us manifest activity, decision and energy; but let them all be guided by that wisdom which selects the best means for the attainment of given ends."

The second annual meeting, held at the State House in Providence, January 7th, 1847, was numerously attended by the friends of education from all parts of the State. It was a goodly company of large hearted and disinterested workers. President Kingsbury was in the chair to congratulate the

Association on the success that had thus far attended the educational enterprise in the State, and to urge "continued action and zeal by which the noble objects in view might be achieved." Dr. Wayland was there to advocate the establishing of district school libraries throughout the State, as was Commissioner Barnard to designate the amount of money necessary to procure them, and to suggest the manner of raising it. William S. Baker, the devoted agent of the INSTITUTE and helpful coadjutor of the State Commissioner, was there, to tell of the old school houses that had been renovated, the new school houses that had been erected, the spirit of inquiry that had been awakened, and the active movements every where visible in the State. Rev. Mr. Vail, of Westerly, Judge Whipple, of Coventry, Dr. Ballou, of Cumberland, and Mr. George Manchester, of Portsmouth, were there, to testify to the happy results of the educational movement in their respective towns. Hon. William Hunter, of Newport, was there, to relate school reminiscences of his early days, and to draw a favorable contrast between 1797 and 1847; and Superintendent Bishop was there, to show how much the enlightened efforts of Rhode Island were appreciated abroad.

Mr. Amos Perry, in behalf of the Executive Committee, presented an able report, comprising a *resumé* of the work of the year. It exhibited practical views of Teachers' Institutes and of the importance of a Normal School. It took elevated ground touching teaching as a profession. It affirmed that "the best talents of the community should be enlisted in the profession of the teacher, and with them should be associated those accomplishments and attractions which give power and influence over mind and character." It closed with an earnest invitation to "the citizens of the State to continue to co-operate in promoting the prosperity of that cause which underlies all the great interests of the State, and is the foundation and pillar upon which rests the broad fabric of our republican institutions—the intelligence and virtue of the people."

A memorial to the legislature was reported and adopted,

4

asking an appropriation for the purchase of volumes of the
"*Journal of the Rhode Island Institute of Instruction,*" to be
placed in the several districts of the State.

The third annual meeting of the Institute, held in the same
place on the evening of January 24th, 1848, was a session of
no less interest and profit, though more thinly attended on
account of strong attractions elsewhere. A valuable and
suggestive report was made in behalf of the Executive Committee, by Mr. Caleb Farnum, and earnest addresses were
made by Messrs. William Gammell, Joseph T. Sisson, Henry
Barnard, Nathan Bishop and Wilkins Updike. A communication from Rev. Mr. Vail, of Westerly, was also read,
giving "a cheering account of the cause of education in his
vicinity." One thousand dollars had been recently raised in
that town for the establishment of a Library.

"Mr. Updike illustrated the progress of education in this State. He
could speak from an extensive observation. He knew the '*District
School as it was,*" in Rhode Island. He had known some of its teachers,
men who were employed without the slightest regard to their qualifications as educators. He had known those employed in the sacred office
of teacher for the very reason that they were unfit for anything else.
They were too stupid, shiftless, and feeble in body and mind to earn their
bread in the ordinary way, and hence were employed to teach school.
He had known a man, an instructor of youth, whose word upon oath was
not to be respected in one of our civil courts. Such teachers, he rejoiced
to say, could not now be found in our schools. A different policy prevails. Teaching is now regarded as a profession, second to none in importance. Those who enter it have to undergo a rigid examination.
They must have a good knowledge of the branches in which they are to
instruct. They must possess a good moral character. They must adopt
improved methods of instruction and discipline. They must devote their
time and their efforts to their schools. The people of Rhode Island no
longer seek the cheapest, but the best men, to train and instruct their
children."

An adjourned meeting of the Institute was held in Westminster Hall, Providence, the week following, (January 25th,)
which was addressed at length by Mr. Barnard, who gave a
detailed statement of the efforts that had been put forth during
the previous four years for the improvement of the public

schools. New schools had been established, new school
houses erected,* and the average amount of school attendance greatly increased.

In concluding his remarks, Mr. Barnard said :

"But let no Rhode Islander forget the immense fund of talent which
has slumbered in unconsciousness, or been only half developed, in the
country towns of this State by reason of the defective provision for general
education. Let the past four years be the first years of a new era—an
era in which education, universal education, the complete and thorough
education of every child born or living in the State, shall be realized.
Let the problem be solved—how much waste by vice and crime can be
prevented, how much the productive power of the State can be augmented,
how far happy homes can be multiplied, by the right cultivation of the
moral nature, and the proportionate development of the intellectual faculties of every child;—how much more, and how much better, the hand
can work when directed by an intelligent mind; how inventions for
abridging labor can be multiplied by cultivated and active thought; in
fine, how a State of one hundred and fifty thousand people can be made
equal to a State of ten times that number; can be made truly an empire
State, ruling by the supremacy of mind and moral sentiments. All this
can be accomplished by filling the State with educated mothers, well
qualified teachers, and good books, and bringing these mighty agencies to
bear directly and under the most favorable circumstances upon every
child and every adult. . . . . Educate well, if you can educate only

---

* In his Report for 1848, Mr. Barnard said: "To Mr. Thomas A. Tefft, of Providence, much credit is due for the taste he has displayed in the designs furnished
by him, and for the elevations which he drew for plans furnished or suggested by
the Commissioner. He should not, however, be held responsible for the altera-
tions made in his plans by the committees and carpenters having charge of the
erections of the buildings after plans furnished by him."

School houses, after Mr. Tefft's designs, were erected in Westerly, Allendale,
Barrington, Warren, Centreville and Providence. The latter is the house built
on Benefit street for the Young Ladies' School, for many years kept by Hon. John
Kingsbury, and now under the charge of Rev. J. C. Stockbridge, D. D. Mr. Tefft
was a native of Richmond, and commenced his career as a school teacher at the
early age of 17 years. He came to Providence and studied architecture with Tallman & Bucklin. He entered Brown University and graduated with the Degree of
B. P. He subsequently visited Europe, and acquainted himself with the various
styles of architecture in England, Scotland, France, Lombardy, Italy and Russia.
While abroad, he perfected a system of Universal Currency, which in its main
features was adopted, though without acknowledgment, by a conference representing nineteen nations, held at Paris in 1867. Mr. Tefft died at Florence, December 12, 1859, after a short illness, in the 34th year of his age.

one sex, the female children, so that every home shall have an educated mother. Bring the mighty stimulus of the living voice and well matured thought on great moral, scientific, literary and practical topics, to bear on the whole community so far as it can be gathered together to listen to popular lectures. Introduce into every town and every family the great and the good of all past time, of this and other countries by means of public libraries of well selected books. And above all, provide for the professional training, the permanent employment, and reasonable compensation of teachers,—and especially of female teachers, for upon their agency in popular education must we rely for a higher style of manners, morals and intellectual culture."

Sentiments like these can never become obsolete.

The meeting was also addressed by Messrs. William Gammell, Osgood and Bishop.

In 1856, Mr. Kingsbury declined re-election as President of the Institute, an office he had held eleven years with great acceptance. These were years of vast importance in the history of the Institute. It was the formative period in the new educational dispensation, and its industry in molding chaotic elements into seemly form was well rewarded. Old errors were brought to light and exploded, new methods were brought forward and established, and a broad, solid foundation was laid, upon which to build a system such as the progress of the age and the needs of the State demanded. Mr. Kingsbury's mature experience as the Principal of a flourishing School for Young Ladies, his extensive acquaintance with the leading educators of the time, whose assistance as lecturers he was able to command, his thorough understanding of the philosophy of education, together with the confidence reposed in his sound judgment, eminently qualified him to give effective direction to the operations of the Institute, and his labors to that end were untiring. To his forecast and active interest the Association is indebted for a fund from the income of which a portion of its annual expenses is defrayed.

On retiring from a position that had been marked by great industry and success, the appreciation of Mr. Kingsbury's services by the Institute was expressed in the following resolution, unanimously adopted :

"*Resolved*, That the thanks of this Institute are hereby given to Mr. John Kingsbury for his long, very able and very faithful services as its first President, and that we heartily congratulate him on the success of his efforts in behalf of our Association, and in the great cause of education, to which the earnest labors of his life have been so efficiently devoted."

Professor Samuel S. Greene, of Brown University, was elected to fill the office vacated by Mr. Kingsbury, and held it four years. During this time he brought many valuable influences to the support of the Institute. He labored earnestly to establish the Normal School on a solid foundation, and to elevate the standard of education, by lectures, addresses, and the stimulus of personal communication with individuals interested in the cause. In this work he was vigorously assisted by Mr. Dana P. Colbourn, whose sudden death by casualty in 1855, awakened sadness throughout Rhode Island, where he was well known and highly esteemed, as it did in the wide circle of friends in other States. Professor Greene retired from the presidency of the Institute in 1860. The successive incumbents to January, 1874, have been John J. Ladd, William A. Mowry, Thomas W. Bicknell, Noble W. DeMunn, James T. Edwards, Albert J. Manchester, and Merrick Lyon.* The distinguishing features of these respective administrations will be seen in the synopsis of meetings given in subsequent pages. Under each president the Institute has continued to prosper. Its value as an educational agent was never more highly estimated than at present.

The educational condition of the State in 1844, as relates to school houses, length of school terms, attendance, etc., is fairly exhibited by the following statements derived from official sources :

* Mr. Isaac F. Cady, an experienced educator, succeeded Mr. Lyon as President, January, 1874.

"As the schools were then organized, four hundred and five school houses were required, whereas but three hundred and twelve were provided. Of these twenty-nine were owned by towns in their corporate capacity; one hundred and forty-seven by proprietors; and one hundred and forty-five by school districts. Of two hundred and eighty houses from which full returns were received, including those in Providence, twenty-five were in very good repair; sixty-two were in ordinary repair; and eighty-six were pronounced totally unfit for school purposes; sixty-five were located in the public highway, and one hundred and eighty directly on the line of the road, without any yard or outbuildings attached; and but twenty-one had a play ground enclosed. In over two hundred school rooms the average height was less than eight feet, without any opening in the ceiling, or other effectual means for ventilation; the seats and desks were calculated for more than two pupils, arranged on two or three sides of the room, and in most instances, where the result of actual measurement was given, the highest seats were over eighteen inches from the floor, and the lowest, except in twenty-five schools, were over fourteen inches for the youngest pupils, and these seats were unprovided with backs. Two hundred and seventy schools were unfurnished with a clock, blackboard, or thermometer, and only five were provided with a scraper and mat for the feet."

These houses were badly lighted, poorly ventilated, and imperfectly warmed. There were no hooks and shelves for garments and hats: no well, sink, basin and towels to secure cleanliness: no places of retirement for children of either sex; and around the houses no verdure, trees, shrubbery and flowers for the eye.

"In some districts an apartment in an old shop or dwelling house was fitted up as a school room; and in eleven towns, the school houses, such as they were, were owned by proprietors, to whom in many instances, the districts paid in rent a larger amount than would have been the interest on the cost of a new and commodious school house."

"The whole number of persons over four and under sixteen years of age, the ordinary but not exclusive subjects of school education, in the different towns in the State, including the city of Providence, was about thirty thousand.

"The whole number of persons of all ages who attended any school, public or private, any portion of the year, was twenty-four thousand. Of this number, twenty-one thousand were enrolled as attending the public schools, and three thousand as receiving instruction at home, or in private schools, of different grades, at periods of the year when the public schools were open. At other periods of the year the number attending private schools, taught by teachers of public schools, was much larger.

"Of the twenty-one thousand connected with the public schools during the year, eighteen thousand only were between the ages of four and sixteen years. One-third of the whole number enrolled, attended school so irregularly, that the average attendance of children of all ages in the public schools, did not exceed thirteen thousand five hundred, or less than one-half of all the children of a proper school age. The number who attended school during the whole year, allowing for vacations of ordinary length, did not exceed five thousand, including scholars in primary schools, while more than six thousand, on an average, did not attend a public school three months in the year. Less than half the whole number of scholars were girls. Of the scholars over sixteen years of age, the proportion of boys to the girls was as five to one. Of the scholars over ten years of age, the number of boys were to the girls as four to one.

"The average length of schools in twenty-seven towns, was about four months. In two hundred and fifty-five school districts, there was but one session of less than four months in the year, leaving a vacation of eight months. In one hundred and sixty-six districts the public schools were open but nine weeks in the year. Upwards of six thousand scholars attended public school less than three months; while less than two thousand children, excluding the scholars in the public schools of Providence, and of those districts where the public schools were kept through the year, attended eight months in the year. The general standard of attainment with scholars over eight years old, in most of the schools visited, was at least three years below what it should have been, if the same scholars had commenced going to school when they were five years of age.

"In ninety-six districts, comprising in the aggregate three thousand eight hundred pupils, less than one thousand were present during the first week, and more than that number did not join until after the close of the third week of the term. In the same district, four hundred and sixty left school three weeks before the term closed. The average length of the school term in these districts, was thirteen weeks. But not only was the nominal length of the school term curtailed in this way, but a portion was clipped both from the opening and close of every day's sessions."

Add to all this the lack of a uniform system of classification, the disregard by pupils of punctuality at the opening of the daily sessions, irregularity in attendance amounting to full one-third of all belonging, the great variety of books used, the crowding of pupils of all ages, capacities, and degrees of advancement into one room, barren of furniture appropriate to either, with a wide-spread indifference, if not positive hostility to change, and the reader will have a clear

idea of the condition and needs of the schools of Rhode
Island when the State Commissioner commenced the work of
improvement.

In 1845, the Institute appointed Mr. William S. Baker, of
South Kingstown, to act as its agent to carry forward the
work and promote the objects it had in view. Mr. Baker's
experience as a teacher, his singleness of purpose, and his
devotion to the cause of popular education, qualified him pre-
eminently for the service assigned him. He entered heartily
into the work, and became an invaluable coadjutor of the
State Commissioner. Under the direction of a committee of
the Institute, he traveled from town to town; conversed with
the people in their homes, in the field, and in the workshop;
visited the schools; held meetings of the parents; and in
every other practicable mode endeavored to awaken an interest in educational improvement. The services he rendered
were of immense advantage, and his name will ever be held
in honor, as one identified with the public school movement
embraced in the period of which we are now speaking.

Mr. Barnard continued actively engaged in the duties of
his office until 1849, when enfeebled health caused him to
tender his resignation. Unable to write out his final report
at the time, he was invited by the legislature to make an
oral communication to the two houses in joint convention, on
the condition and improvement of the public schools. This
address, of two hours duration, fervid and heartfelt in utter-
ance, commanded the undivided attention of the audience, and
the views and facts presented made a deep impression. Both
branches of the General Assembly united in a vote of thanks
to Mr. Barnard for the able, faithful and judicious manner in
which for five years he had fulfilled the duties of Commissioner of Public Schools in the State of Rhode Island. The
teachers of the State, through a committee appointed for the
purpose, presented him with a silver pitcher, as a testimonial
of their respect and friendship, and of their appreciation of
his services in the cause of education.* At the request of a

* This committee consisted of Robert Allyn, Jenks Mowry, Solomon P. Wells,

committee of citizens from different parts of the State, Mr. Barnard sat for his portrait, which was painted by Lincoln, of Providence, and presented to the Rhode Island Historical Society.

During the five years of service by Mr. Barnard, more than eleven hundred meetings were held, expressly to discuss topics connected with the public schools, at which upwards of fifteen hundred addresses were delivered. One hundred and fifty of these meetings continued through the day and evening; upwards of one hundred through two evenings and a day; fifty through two days and three evenings; and twelve, including Teachers' Institutes, through the entire week. In addition to this class of meetings and addresses, upwards of

Fanny J. Burges, Jane Fifield, Sylvester Patterson, and George W. Dodge. In the letter accompanying this gift the committee say:

"Of the extent of your labors in preparing the way for a thorough re-organization of our system of public schools, and in encountering successfully the many difficulties incident to the working of a new system, few of us can probably be aware. But we can speak from a personal knowledge of the value of the Teachers' Institutes which have from time to time been held by your appointment, and provided (too often, we fear, at your expense) with skilful and experienced instructors, and practical lecturers; and of the many books and pamphlets on education and teaching, which you have scattered broadcast over the State.

" We can speak, too, of what the teachers of the state know from daily observation,—many of them from happy experience,—of the great change,—nay, revolution,—which you have wrought in our school architecture; by which old, dilapidated, and unsightly district school houses have given way for the many new, attractive, commodious and healthy edifices which now adorn our hills and valleys. We have seen, too, and felt the benefits of the more numerous and regular attendance of scholars, of the uniformity of text-books, the more vigilant supervision of school committees, and the more lively and intelligent interest and co-operation of parents in our labors, which have been brought about mainly by your efforts.

"The fruits of your labors may also be seen in the courses of popular lectures which are now being held, and in the well-selected town, village and district libraries, which you have assisted in establishing, and which are already scattering their life-giving influence through our beloved State. In the consciousness of having been the main instrumentality in effecting these changes, for'which the generations yet unborn will bless your memory, you have your own best reward. . . . . May your future course be as honorable to yourself, as the past has been useful to the children and youth of Rhode Island."

5

two hundred meetings of teachers and parents were held for
lectures and discussions on improved methods of teaching,
and for public exhibitions or examinations of schools.
Besides these various meetings, experienced teachers were
employed to visit particular towns and sections of the State,
and converse freely with parents, on the condition and improvement of the public schools.   By these agencies a meeting was held within three miles of every home in Rhode
Island.   In addition to all this, more than sixteen thousand
educational pamphlets and tracts were distributed gratuitously
through the State; "and one year not an almanac was sold
in Rhode Island without at least sixteen pages of educational
reading attached." This statement does not include the official
documents published by the State, nor the Journal of the
Institute, nor upwards of twelve hundred bound volumes on
schools and school systems, and the theory and practice of
teaching, purchased by teachers, or added to public and private libraries.*

These years of faithful service had left their impress on the
State.   They had been years of progress, and the sun on the
dial of their record could not go back.   On retiring from a field
so industriously cultivated, Mr. Barnard had the satisfaction of
seeing marked improvement in school houses, in methods of
teaching, and in the tone of the public mind touching the
duties of parents, and the relation of intellectual culture to
the social and material prosperity of the State.

It would be interesting to trace in these pages the progressive steps by which, from 1848 the public schools of Rhode
Island have advanced to their present standing ; but for all purposes of comparison some statistics drawn from the State
Commissioner's reports for 1872 and 1873 will suffice.

In 1872 the whole number of public summer schools in the

* Before Mr. Barnard left the State, a library of at least five hundred volumes
had been secured for twenty nine out of the thirty-two towns. The first district
library established during his official connection with the State was at Portsmouth.

State was 687 ; winter schools, 727 ; pupils in the summer schools, 26,912 ; winter schools, 28,702. Within that year it is believed not less than 34,000 different pupils enjoyed the benefit of public school instruction. The number of male teachers employed in summer was 93 ; in winter, 177 ; female teachers in summer, 616 ; in winter, 579. The amount expended for teachers and school houses was $465,623.63, being an advance of $410,570.63 on the record of 1844. Indeed, the city of Providence expended in 1872, for the support of its schools, $155,000, exclusive of $40,000 expended on school houses. approximating to nearly three times the sum appropriated thirty years ago for the support of all the public schools in the State.

In 1873, the number of public schools in the State was 719. Expenditures for school purposes, including salaries of teachers, $602,812.28. Number of male teachers, 172 ; female. 585. The number of pupils registered in the fall schools, 24,905 ; winter schools, 28,525 : spring schools, 21,919. Number of pupils registered for the entire year, 3 ,448. Percentage of attendance in summer schools, 82 : fall schools, 81 ; winter schools, 79 ; spring schools, 82. Percentage of attendance during the year, 81. Estimated number of children in private and Catholic schools, 8,000 ; instructed at home, 1,000 ; instructed at public and private day schools, or, instructed at home, 38,500.*

In 1873, Providence expended for school purposes, $267,-597.25, or $72,597.25 more than was expended in 1872. Of this sum, $146,656.13 were paid for teachers' salaries. The school returns for the same year show the average monthly salary paid male teachers in the State to have been $75.72 ; the average salary per school year, $677.69. The average salary of female teachers, per month, was $41.97 : the average salary per year, $375.63. The highest salaries were, and continued to be, paid in Providence. These statistics exhibit a commendable advance upon former years, though the com-

---

* State Commissioner's Report for 1873.

pensation for competent services is still less than it should be. The school year of Rhode Island, counting the weeks of actual teaching, is now the longest of any State in New England. That the influence of the *Institute* has largely aided in producing these results, there can be no doubt.

On a preceding page, under consecutive date, it should have been stated that, in 1839, Mr. Nathan Bishop, then a tutor in Brown University, was appointed Superintendent of Public Schools in Providence. The idea of this office originated with Mr. John L. Hughes and Mr. Simon Henry Greene, the former being a member of the school committee, and both members of the Common Council of that city. Its recommendation for adoption was presented to the council in the report of a committee of which Mr. Hughes was chairman, and to whom the subject of reorganizing the school system of the city had been committed. The report bears date September 25, 1837, and is signed by the chairman, Stephen T. Olney, Henry Anthony, Amherst Everett, Seth Padelford, and James E. Butts. The recommendation grew out of private conversations between Mr. Hughes[*] and Mr. Greene, who heartily co-operated in all measures for advancing the interests of the schools; and the advantages derived from incorporating this office into the revised system of education became at an early day so obvious, that the example was soon followed by Boston, and in successive years by the cities of other States in the Union. In Rhode Island every town is now, under authority of statute law, provided with a school superintendent. "The practical value of this important school officer to each town, has proved the wisdom of the law creating the office."[†]

---

[*] Mr. Hughes was a son of Major Thomas Hughes, a brave and highly esteemed officer of the Revolution. He gave a hearty support to the cause of public education, and the inclusion of a High School in the plan of public instruction in Providence, in 1838, was largely due to his exertions.

[†] State Commissioner's Report, 1873.

Mr. Barnard's Successors.

On the retirement of Mr. Barnard from the office of State School Commissioner, Hon. ELISHA R. POTTER, of Kingston, was appointed his successor. His extensive acquaintance throughout the State ensured him ready access to many persons of influence, whose co-operation was desirable, while his legal knowledge qualified him to decide promptly all questions brought to his attention on appeal.

One of the most useful services rendered to the schools by Mr. Potter consisted in making the law relating to them familiar to the people. It was almost entirely a new system. True, there were districts before, but the change was very great. The powers of districts and of school officers were very much increased and attempted to be defined. It was the introduction of a great deal of new machinery, of course involving considerable friction. The largest portion of the remarks intended to elucidate the law, and the forms to facilitate the business of officers under it, had been prepared by Mr. Potter before that, and without doubt his exertions resulted in preventing, by anticipation, much of the ill-feeling which would have ended in law-suits, and which when once excited in a district, would have retarded the progress of the schools for years.*

Another feature of Mr. Potter's administration was a movement to awaken a taste for the study of Natural History in the higher grades of schools, a study in which few at that

---

* At the January session of the General Assembly, 1873, a committee consisting of Hon. Elisha R. Potter, Associate Justice of the Supreme Court, Hon. Thomas W. Bicknell, State Commissioner of Public Schools, and Hon. Joshua M. Addeman, Secretary of State, was appointed to cause to be printed a Manual containing the school laws of Rhode Island, for the use of school committees, trustees of school districts, and other officers or persons concerned in the administration of public schools. It makes a neat volume of 284 pages, and will be found very convenient or reference.

time were interested. For this purpose he made engage-
ments with Professor Benoit Jaeger, an eminent naturalist,
to deliver lectures before Teachers' Institutes, held in different
parts of the State. Professor Jaeger was an accomplished
scholar, and by extensive travels, and scientific research, was
thoroughly qualified for the duty assigned him, while his
enthusiasm and fund of illustrative anecdotes, imparted to
his lectures a charm which gained for him, whenever he
spoke, a numerous and attentive audience. To these labors
may be attributed much of the interest in Natural History
since manifested in Rhode Island.*

In his final report to the General Assembly, January, 1854,
Mr. Potter recommended the establishing of a BOARD OF
EDUCATION, as a means of "concentrating the efforts and
exertions of those who would be disposed to take an active
part in promoting the cause of education." He also submit-
ted a bill for that purpose, but for reasons unnecessary to

---

* Professor Jaegar was a native of Austria, and of noble parentage. He was
born in Vienna, and after graduating at the University of that city, entered the
service of the Emperor Alexander of Russia, as Naturalist and lecturer in the
University of St. Petersburg. After the decease of that monarch, he, by direction
of the Czar Nicholas, explored the Crimea, a region then but little known, and to
which he gave the name of *Trans Caucasia*. His report on the natural riches of
that country was published at Leipsic in 1830. He subsequently explored St.
Domingo. On retiring from the imperial service he came to the United States,
and was for nine years Professor of Natural History and Modern Languages in
Princeton College. When a National Scientific Institution, to be established in
Washington, was projected, he was offered and accepted a Professorship in his
favorite departments of Zoology, Entomology and Botany, but the Smithson
bequest led to an abandonment of the original scheme, and after a residence of
several years at Alexandria, Va., he became interested in a private Academy in
New Jersey, and afterwards opened a Polytechnic School on Staten Island, N. Y.
This institution failing of anticipated success, he, in 1859, took up his abode in
Providence, and after a residence of five years in that city, removed to Brooklyn,
N. Y., where he died in the eighty-third year of his age. He was the author of a
Hand Book of Zoology, designed for the use of common schools and academies,
and of " The Life of North American Insects," which passed through two editions.
Professor Jaeger's genial temperament, varied knowledge, and extensive personal
acquaintance with contemporary *savants* in Europe and America, rendered his
conversations alike interesting and instructive.

mention, the recommendation was not adopted. The subject at different times engaged the attention of the Institute, but it was not until 1870, that the proposed measure became a law.

As a means of communicating more frequently with the public, than could be done through annual reports, Mr. Potter, in 1852, commenced the publication of the *"Rhode Island Educational Magazine."* This became the repository of school documents, changes in school laws, decisions on the construction of the law, information of educational meetings and their proceedings, and such other reading matter as would interest and instruct. This magazine was supported principally by the private contributions of gentlemen interested in advancing the cause to which it was devoted, and was sent gratuitously to the chairmen and clerks of school committees, and to the clerk of every school district. In this manner important information was widely diffused and much good accomplished.

When Mr. Potter retired from office in 1854, the appointing power found a competent successor in Rev. ROBERT ALLYN, of East Greenwich. The three years of his administration were industriously improved, and much was done by him towards building up a healthy public sentiment on the subject of education. His reports to the General Assembly contained many practical suggestions, the results of careful observation and reflection. His views of the education of females are worthy of being repeated. He said:

" The education of females is of quite as much importance as that of males. For from these, we must, as our statistics show, recruit the ranks of our teachers, and from the nature of the case, these females must be the guides and instructors of the earliest and most impressible years, of each person in the coming generation. If the teachers, the nurses, and the mothers of any people are ignorant and unrefined, are degraded and vicious, or tending to become so, it is in vain to hope for brave, intelligent, moral, and high-minded sons. On the other hand, if the mothers and teachers are learned and virtuous, enlightened and elevated in sentiment, their sons cannot fail, in most instances, to be worthy of the noble women who bore and instructed them. We ought then to give more attention to this subject of the education of girls—especially among the poorer class, and in the country towns; and we should be particularly careful to see that the girls shall not be deprived of their proper share of school privileges, simply because they make better nurses for younger children, or more profitable assistants in the kitchens than boys do; or because it is erroneously taken for granted, that they do not need so good an education, since they are not designed to carry on machine shops, or conduct the barter of trade and commerce, or to manage the affairs of the national administration. They are to bring up and to educate the men of the nation, and to carry on all the complicated and beneficial operations of our household, and these very necessary and important affairs require not only skill and common sense, but also education and discipline. Let the girls be educated, therefore, quite as numerously and as thorough in our schools as the boys, if we would derive the largest profit from our system of public instruction."

Of the qualities that should be found in teachers, Mr. Allyn spake as follows:

" Let but a bit of iron, of the proper temper, be brought into contact with a powerful magnet, or be placed in a proper position in relation to a current of electricity, and it will itself become magnetic, to the full capacity of its nature; and if properly placed afterwards, will never lose that magnetic character. So it is with men, but especially so with children. Let them be brought into close contact with a strong mind, and they feel its power, and imbibe its peculiar characteristics. They cannot avoid imitating its habits and manners, and they must be molded and shaped and magnetized by its influence. It is therefore of the highest consequence to our schools and to our system of public education, to seek such strong men and women—strong in goodness and in purity, strong in all truthful and noble qualities of manliness and womanliness—to be the teachers of our growing children. We must insist that these teachers shall be not only educated, but that they shall be polished, refined, loving, wise, and philanthropic; that they shall have superadded to every thing that can be learned, or that is native, something even higher than that boasted common sense, without which man is always a blunderer—a nameless something that makes men more than simply teachers, by giving to them a power to impress and elevate, by the force of a character seen and felt, but not to be described, a something that goes out of them, as heat goes out of a fire, or light out of a glowing lamp, no man knows how or why, but with a power that cannot be resisted; a something that silently steals its way into the hearts of all in its neighborhood, imperceptibly and lovingly as magnetic influences creep over the individual particles in a mass of iron filings, and, without affecting in any way, their nature or substance, change them all, from apparently dead matter, into things with life that longs to love, embrace, and adore the polarizing body. These are the influences we must seek in our schools, and we must look for the teachers who can exert them."*

In 1857, Mr. Allyn retired from the post he had usefully and satisfactorily filled. His successor was Hon. JOHN KINGSBURY, whose previous experience as a successful educator, and whose knowledge of the condition of the State, acquired while President of the Institute, well qualified him for the place he was called to fill. He began his work by a tour of inspection. He went from town to town and district to district, until he had visited every school in the State. These visits were usually made in company with some school officer, or some other person in the town interested in the public schools. In riding from one district to another favorable opportunity was afforded for free consultation upon every topic and feature of the school system, for explaining more fully the meaning of the school law, for suggesting methods of settling difficulties, and overcoming obstacles where they existed, and for obtaining such knowledge of the status of the schools as would be helpful in remedying evils and pointing out ways for improvement. The work so faithfully and thoroughly done, contributed to advance the welfare of the schools. In his report to the General Assembly, Mr. Kingsbury gave an encouraging view of the work, together with practical suggestions in regard to the examination of teachers, the improvement of school houses, the furnishing and changing of school books, and other topics. In speaking of the influence of schools, he says :

"Good schools will add to the pecuniary value of farms and other property, in their immediate neighborhood; but what is of far greater consequence, they will raise the standard of intellectual and moral ex-

* With the close of Mr. Potter's administration, the *Educational Magazine* ceased to exist. At the annual meeting of the Institute in 1854, it was voted to establish the *Rhode Island Schoolmaster*, and Mr. Allyn was appointed its editor.

cellence. The welfare of children should never be weighed in the scales of pecuniary gain or loss. There is something infinitely higher and better than money—and *that* is character."

His opinion of the Normal School, which had then been organized about four years, he thus expresses :

"My visitation enables me to bear strong testimony in favor of the training and instruction which are given in our Normal School. I am convinced that it is an instrumentality in the cause of public schools which cannot be, at present, rightly estimated. The time is not far distant, however, when the people of the State will feel that no money for the promotion of education, is more wisely expended than that which is appropriated to the support of the Normal School. They will see that from such an expenditure they are themselves to reap special blessings which are to come into their own households. This is not the work of a day. Time must be given, not only for the tree to be planted, but also for its fruit to come to maturity. If it were otherwise, it would be contrary to the analogy of other human institutions."

In all his work Mr. Kingsbury received the hearty co-operation of the Institute.

Mr. Kingsbury was succeeded in 1859 by Dr. JOSHUA B. CHAPIN, who, with an interregnum of two years, held the office until 1869. His eight years of service covered a period in which the distracted state of the public mind caused by the Rebellion, affected all interests. From the consequences of an absorbing anxiety for the salvation of the nation, which, like Aaron's rod, swallowed up almost every other thought, the public schools could not be expected wholly exempt. But though many excellent teachers withdrew for a time from their profession and entered the Union army, and a very considerable draft was made upon children and youth of school age, to supply the places in factories, vacated by adults who had in like manner enlisted, the schools suffered less than might reasonably have been supposed, and it is gratifying to notice that during the five years of intestine war, the reports show a gradual improvement in their condition. Dr. Chapin pursued the course of his predecessors in visiting the several school districts, noticing the general condition of schools and school houses, observing the methods of discipline and instruction, and offering such suggestions and remarks as the circumstances seemed to require. He also addressed meetings of the citizens upon various topics of educational interest. In his several reports he urged the necessity of parental co-operation with teachers—frequent visits to the schools by parents and committees,—a careful selecting of sites for school houses, so as to secure ample grounds around them,— care in the choice and appointment of teachers,—encouraging music in all our schools for its refining influence in the cultivation of moral and social character, as well as an aid in discipline,—a large experience and high qualities of mind and character in teachers of Primary schools, for the reason that no department of instruction suffers more than this from inattention. He affirmed that our Primary schools are of primary importance,—that foundations laid here must modify, as well as sustain, the entire superstructure,—that the temple cannot be broader than its base,—and that it is not enough in these schools to make right impressions; they should be made in the right way. In his report in 1864, he advocated a liberal policy in the compensation of teachers, in order to secure for the schools the best quality of teaching talent, in these words :

"No man can be expected to give his life for less than what will enable him to live. No man expects to secure able and faithful agents in other departments of business if he does not sufficiently compensate them. The shrewd manufacturer bids high for skillful labor, and so with the mechanic and the artizan. The anxious father employs the best medical aid for his sick son, and expects to pay for it. The embarrassed client consults the most learned counsel. and he expects the fee to be, in some degree, the measure of the value of the service which he receives. No congregation hopes to secure the services of a 'popular divine' without the payment of a liberal salary. And no parent who is not culpably indifferent to the educational interests of his children, would think of limiting the wages of the schoolmaster to less than those of the common day laborer. . . . . Parents have no claim upon the services of a good teacher. who are unwilling to pay the frugal expenses of such a teacher, and to remunerate him for the time, labor and cost of securing his educational qualifications."

HENRY ROUSMANIERE, Esq., of Cranston, became the successor of Dr. Chapin, in 1861, and continued in office two years, when the latter again received the appointment of Commissioner.   Mr. Rousmaniere commenced his work after the manner of his predecessors, by a survey of the field he was to occupy.   In the first six months of his administration he made more than three hundred visits to different districts, to make himself "acquainted personally with the practical working of our system of education."

Mr. Rousmaniere's views of the work of true education are expressed in the following extracts from his report for 1863 :

"True education aims at the growth of the body and mind; neither to be so developed as to disturb the harmony of the other; and both to kneel in homage to the moral faculty.

"Right education secures the health of the physical system through the laws of endurance and activity; stimulates the imagination to a sense of the grand and beautiful in art and nature; awakens the understanding to acquaintance with the practical problems of the age; guides the reason to lift itself higher than the plane of the senses; vivifies the affections to a love of truth rather than self; true wisdom rather than mere book learning; eternity rather than time."

In 1869, Hon. THOMAS W. BICKNELL, of Barrington, succeeded Dr. Chapin in the office of State Commissioner.   He brought to its duties a valuable preparation drawn from an experience of several years as a teacher in Grammar and High Schools, combined with an earnest purpose.   In the outset he made a careful survey of the State, thus informing himself of the actual condition and needs of every town and school district.   His early effort was, by frequent private conversations and public addresses, to awaken among the people a hearty interest in the work of school advancement. In the five years that Commissioner Bicknell has held the office, his activity in the discharge of his duties has been unremitting, and the scope of his thought and labors is well indicated by the various topics embraced in his annual reports to the General Assembly.   Feeling, at the beginning, the need of a Normal School, as a means of ensuring to the

schools of the State teachers of broad and liberal culture, and
also of a State Board of Education, which " would concentrate its influence and exertions to promote the healthy growth
of our public schools," he recommended their establishment
to the General Assembly.   To this recommendation that
body cordially responded, and both the School and the Board
were established by law ; the latter coming into existence in
1870, and the former in 1871.*   In addition to conducting,
as editor-in-chief, the *Rhode Island Schoolmaster*, attending
and participating in the meetings of the RHODE ISLAND IN-
STITUTE OF INSTRUCTION, the Commissioner has continued,
year by year, a series of local visitations, besides holding
numerous independent Institute meetings in different parts
of the State, for the benefit of teachers, and for the purpose
of strengthening school interests in the hearts of parents and
guardians of youth.   In the same time a system of meetings
of town and city school superintendents for consultation and
interchange of opinions, has been established, a broad foundation for a State educational library, for the use of the Commissioner's office has been laid, generous appropriations from
the General Assembly for various educational purposes have
been secured, and many other things done to advance the
cause   In review of the year 1873, the Board of Education
say :

" In the survey of the work, and its results for the past year, the Board
have abundant reason to congratulate the General Assembly on the advance that has been made in the cause of popular education. The rich
fruitage of the earnest and faithful labors of our indefatigable Commissioner, are becoming more and more manifest every year."

In bringing this brief notice to a close, the following ex-
tract from the Commissioner's report for 1870, entitled " *The
Education We Need*," will be regarded as pertinent :

" Every child in the State is entitled to a good common school educa-

* Further notice of the Normal School will be found in another part of this
work.

tion. The State Constitution guarantees this, as a fundamental right, preparatory to the large and responsible duties of the citizen and elector. The twelfth article of our State Constitution declares, that the diffusion of knowledge as well as of virtue among the people, being essential to the preservation of their rights and liberties, it shall be the duty of the General Assembly to promote public schools, and to adopt all means which they may deem necessary and proper to secure to the people the advantages and opportunities of education. To fulfil these declarations, free schools have been established, and so far as they have accomplished their proper and legitimate work, have aided in preserving the rights and liberties of the people. A public school system was established, and has been maintained, with variable measures of success, in exact correspondence to the amount of interest, zeal, and labor which was infused into it by school officers, teachers and patrons. A perfect system may become a perfect failure if it does not feel the vital forces pervading it which spring from the popular will. An imperfect system may be made to do wonders if its defects are supplemented by an intelligent and enthusiastic body of workers, supporting and advancing its interests. To secure such a hearty coöperation from the whole people, the working plan must touch and vitalize every interest, and in its broad and liberal provisions it must meet the present and anticipate the prospective wants of every child and every man in society. A noted king and philosopher of ancient times, when asked what kind of an education should be given to boys, answered, 'That kind of knowledge they will need to use when they become men.'

"A system of free schools to be universally popular must be universally practical, so much so that the dullest comprehension may see something of intrinsic value in it. It becomes every intelligent citizen and legislator, therefore, to inquire to what extent the operations of the system meet the wants of the people, and wherein it fails to secure the desired end. The answers to their inquiries will suggest the methods of removing the difficulties which actually exist, in giving a good education to all the youths in our State."

Synopsis of Institute Meetings.

Having thus noticed the administration of each State School Commissioner, whose work was inseparably associated with that of the RHODE ISLAND INSTITUTE OF INSTRUCTION, we turn once more to the records of the Institute, and present therefrom a synopsis of its proceedings as indicating its spirit and the direction of its labors.

On the 24th of January, 1845, was held the *first meeting* of the Institute, W. Updike in the chair. The committee reported favorably on the draft of a Constitution prepared by Mr. Barnard, which was adopted. After remarks upon "The General Interests of Education in Rhode Island," by Messrs. H. Barnard, F. Wayland, A. Caswell, C. Farnum, S. Osgood, J. T. Sisson, N. Bishop, and C. G. Perry, a committee was appointed to nominate officers.

Second Meeting.—January 28th, 1845 at Providence.

An election of officers was made, and John Kingsbury chosen the first President of the Institute.

Prof. Gammell offered resolutions commendatory of the objects of the Institute, which were discussed by Messrs. L. Haile, J. S. Pitman, H. Day, C. Farnum, H. Barnard, N. Bishop, G. L. Dwight, and Rev. Mr. Waterman.

Third Meeting.—February 19th, 1845, at East Greenwich.

Addresses upon "The Educational Wants of Rhode Island," by W. Updike and H. Barnard.

Remarks upon "The Importance of Education," by S. Vernon and J. Durfee.

Fourth Meeting.—February 28th and March 1st and 2d, 1845, at Woonsocket.

Addresses upon "The Condition of Schools in Rhode Island," by W. Updike and H. Barnard; "The Evils of a Mis-directed Education," by H. Barnard.

Discussions upon "School Houses; their location, construction, &c.," by Messrs. J. B. Tallman, C. Farnum, S. S. Greene, W. A. Steere, A. Harkness, J. Kingsbury, J. D. Giddings, and H Barnard; "The Causes of Failure in Teaching," by J. Kingsbury; "Method of Teaching Spelling," by Messrs. Barnard, Farnum, G. C. Wilson, T. Davis, and S. Bushee; "Method of Teaching Reading," by Messrs. Barnard, Farnum, Giddings, and others; "Music as a Branch of Education in Schools," by Messrs. S. W. Coggshall, Tallman, Giddings, and Barnard; "Means of Securing Regularity and Punctuality of Attendance," by Rev. J. Boyden; "Methods of Conducting School Examinations," by H. Barnard.

Fifth Meeting.—June 25th and 26th, 1845, at Newport.

Addresses by Messrs. Gammell, Thayer, L. B. Smith, Brooks, Barnard, F. Brown, E. Clark, Terry, and J. S. Tourtellott.

Sixth Meeting.—September 12th, 1845, at Warren.

Discussions upon school subjects, by Messrs. Barnard, T. R. Hazard, Dr. Moore, Hathaway, J. P. Tustin, and others.

Addresses upon "The Connection Between Common School Education and State Prosperity," by Prof. Gammell; "How Parents may Second the Efforts of Teachers," by Rev. T. Shepard; "Methods of Securing Regular Attendance of Pupils," by A. Perry, followed by Messrs. Barnard, Tustin, and others.

Seventh Meeting.—September 19th and 20th, 1845, at Valley Falls.

Remarks upon "A Plan of Gradation for Schools," by Messrs. Barnard and Bishop; "Stability of Population Promoted by Good Schools," by T. M. Burgess; "Punctuality and Regularity of Attendance, by Messrs. H. Day and J. T. Sisson.

Discussions on "Methods of Managing and Disciplining Schools," by Messrs. G. A. Willard, Crowell, J. B. Tallman, Sisson, Kingsbury, Farnum, Gay, Harkness, Giddings, Wilkinson, Benson and T. Davis; "Methods of Improvement of the Schools of the Village," by Messrs. Kingsbury, Bishop and Day.

Eighth Meeting.—September 26th and 27th, 1845, at Chepachet.

Addresses on "The Public Schools the Only Available Means of a General Education," by J. Kingsbury; "The Importance of Moral Education," by Rev. Mr. Cheney; "My Experience as a Pupil and a Teacher," by C. Farnum; "The Importance of a Radical Change in our System of Public Education," by H. Barnard, followed by Messrs. Perry, D. G. Grosvenor, and Tourtellot.

Ninth Meeting.—September 30th, 1845, at Olneyville.

Address on "On Schools Good Enough for the Rich, and Cheap Enough for the Poor," by H. Barnard.

Discussions by Messrs. Farnum, Day and Harkness.

Remarks on the Importance of Paying Respect to the Teacher's Office," by O. Angell.

Tenth Meeting.—October 4th, 1845, at Pawtuxet.

Addresses "On the Importance of the Gradation of Schools," by N. Bishop and H. Barnard; on "Uniformity of Education Necessary to Solid Equilibrium," by Rev. Mr. Osgood.

Remarks on "The Warming of School-houses," by Messrs. Hartshorn, and Barnard.

Eleventh Meeting.—October 7th, 1845, at Fruit Hill.

Addresses by Messrs. Kingsbury, Bishop, Day, Harkness, and Belden.

Twelfth Meeting.—October 10th, 1845, at Scituate.

Addresses by Messrs. Kingsbury, E. W. Baker, and Rev H. Quimby.

Thirteenth Meeting.—October 14th, 1845, at Foster, Hemlock Village.

Addresses by Messrs. Kingsbury, Barnard, and others; on "Town Libraries," by H. Barnard.

Fourteenth Meeting.—October 30th, 1845, at Kingston.

Address on "The Value of a Good Education in a Commercial Point of View," by Dr. Wayland.

Remarks on "Educational Wants and Defects," by Messrs. Kingsbury, and W. S. Baker; "The Proper Construction of School-houses," by Messrs. Colgrove and Vernon; "The Means and Importance of Securing Good Teachers," by Messrs. Goodwin, Davis, and Baker; "The Means of Increasing the Effectiveness of Schools in the Coming Winter," by H. Barnard.

Fifteenth Meeting.—December 19th and 20th, 1845, at Bristol.

Addresses upon "Punctuality," and other subjects, by Messrs. Kingsbury, N. B. Cook, T. Shepard, Sykes, J. Gushee, Bosworth, Bishop, and Barnard.

Discussions upon "Methods of Discipline and Instruction."

Sixteenth Meeting.—SECOND ANNUAL MEETING.—January 15th, 1846, at Providence.

Reports from the Treasurer and Executive Committee; Election of Officers.

Remarks by Messrs. T. Shepard, W. Russell, of Boston, Dr. Wayland, Vernon, Updike, Bishop, Caswell, Barnard, and others.

Seventeenth Meeting.—January 30th and 31st, 1846, at Pawtucket.

Remarks on "Who Should be Employed as Public School Teachers?" by N. Bishop; "The Rights of Children to an Education," by H. Day; "The Duty of Parents in Regard to School Discipline," by Dr. Carpenter.

Discussions on "Neatness in School-houses," by Messrs. G. C. Wilson, G. A. Willard, Giddings, Wickes, and Sisson; "The Classification of Schools and Use of Monitors," by Messrs. Barnard, Giddings, Perry, Wilkinson, Benson and Wickes; "The Value of Female Teachers," by Messrs. Barnard, Blodgett, Rounds, Willard, Wilkinson and Boyden; "The Use of the Bible as a School Book," by Messrs. J. Boyden, Hyde, Blodgett, Rounds, Willard, Farnsworth, Wickes, Perry, and Farnum; "Corporal Punishment," by Messrs. Day, Farnum, Perry, Willard, Sisson, Wilson Rounds, Benson and Barnard.

Addresses by Messrs. Willard, Sisson and Barnard.

Eighteenth Meeting.—THIRD ANNUAL MEETING.—January 7th, 1847, at Providence.

Reports from the Treasurer and Executive Committee; Election of Officers.

Resolved, on motion of Dr. Wayland, that the Board of the Institute take measures to promote the establishment of District School Libraries through the State.

A committee was appointed to memorialize the legislature for an appropriation for the purpose of distributing the *Journal of the Rhode Island Institute of Instruction* to the districts.

Remarks on "The Improvements Effected in the Schools of Rhode Island," by Messrs. T. H. Vail, Whipple, A. Ballou, A. J. Manchester, Baker, Bishop, and Hunter.

Nineteenth Meeting.—February 6th, 1847, at Smithfield.

Address by W. Updike.

Discussion on "Methods of Government Available in the Country," by Messrs. Farnum, Giddings, and Harkness.

Lecture on Elocution, by F. Russell.

Twentieth Meeting.—February 19th, 1847, at Apponaug Village.

Addresses by Messrs. Kingsbury, Updike, Baker, and Barnard.

Lesson on Elocution, by F. Russell.

Twenty-first Meeting.—February 20th, 1847, at Knightsville.

7

Addresses by Messrs. Barnard, Baker, Kingsbury and Updike.

Lecture on Elocution, by F. Russell.

Drill of the pupils of W. S. Baker, in Elocution and Arithmetic.

Twenty-second Meeting.—February 27th, 1847, at Johnston.

Addresses by Messrs. Kingsbury, Harkness, Whiting, Waterman, Baker, and Updike.

Twenty-third Meeting.—March 19th, 1847, at Crompton Mills.

Address by Mr. Whitney.

Discussions.

Exercises in Geography, Arithmetic, Singing, &c., by the scholars of several neighboring schools, by Mr. Baker.

Twenty-fourth Meeting.—September 11th, 1847, at Chepachet, on the occasion of the dedication of a new school building.

Address on " Architecture as Connected with Education," by J. Kingsbury; "The Advantages of a Good Education to Individuals and the Community," by Dr. Wayland.

Remarks on " The Relations of Parents and Teachers," by Messrs. Bishop, Fowle, and Brown.

Twenty-fifth Meeting.—FOURTH ANNUAL MEETING.—January 21st and 25th, 1848, at Providence.

Reports from the Treasurer and Executive Committee.

Remarks on " Progress of Education in Rhode Island," by Messrs. Vail, Updike, Sisson, Barnard and Bishop; "Town Libraries and Popular Lectures," by Mr. Osgood; " The Duties of Parents to their Schools," by N. Bishop.

Address on " The Progress and Condition of Schools in Rhode Island," by H. Barnard.

Twenty-sixth Meeting.—At Newport.

Remarks on " The Condition of Schools," by Messrs. Updike, Weeden, Barnard and Whipple.

Twenty-seventh Meeting.—FIFTH ANNUAL MEETING.—January 29th, 1849, at Providence.

Report of Executive Committee; Election of Officers.

Resolved, on motion of Prof. Gammell, (discussed on the two previous meetings,) that Education in Rhode Island will need the fostering care of the legislature, the continued attention of our efficient Commissioner, and the hearty cooperation of all classes of citizens.

Remarks on " The Condition and Statistics of Education in the State," by H. Barnard; " Female Teachers," by Messrs. Bishop, and Baker; " The Condition of Schools," by Messrs. Porter, Hartshorn, and Hall.

Twenty-eighth Meeting.—February 5th, 1849, at Providence.

Address on " The Origin of the Public Schools of Providence," by E. M. Stone.

Remarks on " The Condition of Schools," by Messrs. Clark, Barber, Baker, Cranston and S. Patterson; " The Need of Evening Schools in Providence," by E. M. Stone.

A committee appointed (Messrs. Hartshorn, Dumont, Shepard, Updike, and Harris) to prepare a statement respecting the school fund, and memoralize the people upon the importance of leaving it intact.

Voted, unanimously, that the president express to Mr. Barnard, on his resignation of the office of Commissioner of Public Schools, the high sense entertained by the Institute, of his labors in behalf of the Institute and of the State.

Twenty-ninth Meeting.—SIXTH ANNUAL MEETING.—January 18th and 24th, 1850, at Providence.

Election of officers.

Address on "A Normal School in Connection with Brown University," by N. Bishop, with remarks by Dr. Wayland and others.

Resolutions approving of the establishment of a State Normal School, recommending monthly meetings from October to March, with lectures, &c.

Thirtieth Meeting.—February 1st, 1850, at Providence.

Lecture on "The Duties and Qualifications of Teachers," by W. D. Swan, with remarks by Messrs. Kingsbury, Bishop, Mowry and others.

Thirty-first Meeting.—March 8th, 1850, at Providence.

Address on "Guyot's Physical Geography," by J. Kingsbury, followed by Messrs. Perry and Goodwin.

Thirty-second Meeting—October 18th, 1850, at Providence.

Address on "The Brain," by Dr Ray.

Thirty-third Meeting.—November 1st, 1850, at Providence.

Address on "The True Teacher," by J. D. Philbrick.

Thirty-fourth Meeting.—January 17th, 1851, at Providence.

Address on "The Relations of Parents to their Children in Regard to Education," by N. Bishop.

Remarks on "The Condition of the Poor Children of Providence," by various speakers.

Thirty-fifth Meeting.—SEVENTH ANNUAL MEETING.—February 9th, 1851, at Providence.

Report from the Treasurer; Officers elected.

Lecture on "The Facilities enjoyed by Rhode Island for Promoting Civilization, by Dr. Wayland.

Thirty-sixth Meeting.—EIGHTH ANNUAL MEETING.—January 23d, 1852, at Providence.

Election of Officers.

Address on "The Harmony of Public Schools with our Institutions," by Dr. Sears.

Thirty-seventh Meeting.—February 20th, 1852, at Providence.

Lecture on "Drawing," by Prof. Whitaker.

Thirty-eighth Meeting.—March 19th, 1852, at Providence.

Address on "Geography," by Guyot.

Thirty-ninth Meeting.—April 2d. 1852, at Providence.

Address on "Teaching Arithmetic," by D. P. Colburn.

Fortieth Meeting.—NINTH ANNUAL MEETING.—January 19th, 1853, at Providence.

Election of Officers.

Address on "The Need of Compulsory Laws for Attendance at School," by J. Bates; "School Instruction in Manners," by G. H. Tillinghast.

Forty-first Meeting.—TENTH ANNUAL MEETING.—January 17th, 1854, at Providence.

Election of Officers.

Address on "Educational Progress, and the Need of a Board of Education," by J. Kingsbury, with remarks by Messrs. S. S. Greene, E. R. Potter, A. Perry, and E. M. Stone, upon a State Normal School. Moral and Physical Education, and School Examinations.

Report from G. H. Tillinghast advising the use of a text-book, entitled the "Morals of Manners."

Remarks on "Reading," by Mr. Sumner, of the Normal School.

Forty-second Meeting.—ELEVENTH ANNUAL MEETING.—January 24th, 25th and 26th, 1855, at Providence.

Reports from the Treasurer and Executive Committee; Officers elected.

Address on "The Unconscious Tuition of the Teacher, by F. D. Huntington.

Lectures on "Methods for Promoting Intellectual Culture by the Teachers," by D. P. Colburn; "Physical Geography," by Prof. Guyot; "Manner of Teaching Physical Geography," by Prof. Guyot; "The Relation of the State to Popular Education," by Dr. Sears; "Reading," by Dr. Sears; "The Influence of the Earth's Form upon Human Development," by Prof. Guyot; "The Glaciers of Switzerland," by Prof. Guyot.

Resolution- recommending the establishment of free public evening schools in the manufacturing villages and larger towns; moved by S. Austin, and discussed by Messrs. Stone, Greene, Tillinghast and Arnold: —that, in Normal Schools, instruction in the art of teaching should be the main object, and that a high standard of culture should be a pre-requisite to admission; reported by a committee, and discussed by Messrs. Perry, Vail, Willard, Nash, Greene, Stone, and Colburn;—recommending the establishment of an educational journal under the supervision of the Commissioner, and referring the subject to his action; reported by a committee, and discussed by Messrs. Perry, and Vail;— welcoming the new Commissioner of Public Schools, Rev. Robert Allyn.

Forty-third Meeting.—TWELFTH ANNUAL MEETING.—January 24th and 25th, 1856, at Providence.

Election of Officers; S. S. Greene elected President, J. Kingsbury declining a reelection.

Addresses on "The Importance of Thorough Elementary Instruction," by A. R. Pope; "The Value of the Popular Educator to the Community," by W. W Hoppin; "The Varied Duties of a Faithful Teacher," by Rt. Rev. T. M Clark; "Educational Progress in Rhode Island," by J. Kingsbury.

Resolutions of thanks to J. Kingsbury for his able, faithful, and long continued services.

A committee reported favorably respecting the *Rhode Island Schoolmaster*, and a corresponding committee for that journal, was appointed.

Messrs. Leach, Allyn, and Stone were appointed to coöperate with the legislature in obtaining facts respecting truancy and vagrancy. Discussion by Messrs. Allyn, Leach, Stone, Cook, Boyden, Grosvenor, and others.

Report from a committee recommending to the attention of teachers a book entitled, "Morals of Manners," by Miss C. M. Sedgwick.

Forty-fourth Meeting.—THIRTEENTH ANNUAL MEETING.—January 31st, 1857, at Providence.

Report from the Treasurer; Election of Officers.

Messrs. Greene and Stone appointed to solicit from the General Assembly an appropriation in favor of the *Rhode Island Schoolmaster*.

Forty-fifth Meeting.—May 28th and 29th, 1857, at Newport.

Addresses on "Education," by G. H. Calvert; "The Chief Defects of Home Education," by Rev. W. Burton; "Mathematical Studies," by Rev. W. Stow.

Remarks on "The Advantages of the Social Position of the Teacher," by W. Burton; "The duties of Teachers in the Government and Moral Training of Children," by Messrs. Allyn, Colburn, Burton and Tenney.

Discussion on "Capacity to Govern Without Corporal Punishment, the Highest Qualification of the Teacher," by Messrs. Hazard, Allyn, Stow, and Burton.

Forty-sixth Meeting.—FOURTEENTH ANNUAL MEETING.—February 6th, 1858, at Providence.

Election of Officers; Report of the Treasurer; balance on hand, $1,141.16.

Resolutions recommending the farther increase of evening schools, and free public libraries; on motion of S. Austin, seconded by Rev. E. M. Stone.

Messrs. Greene and Leech were appointed to arrange with the Commissioner for meetings of the Institute in different parts of the State.

[The Records of *six* meetings are not preserved, and all the following numbers are increased by that number.]

Fifty-third Meeting.—FIFTEENTH ANNUAL MEETING.—February 27th, 1859, at Providence.

Report of the Treasurer; Election of Officers.

The Commissioner of Public Schools reported meetings of the Institute during the year at North Foster, Chepachet, Crompton, Mashassuc, and two at Valley Falls.

Address on "Education in the Home," by Rev. W. Barber.

Fifty-fourth Meeting.—SIXTEENTH ANNUAL MEETING.—January 20th and 21st, 1860, at Providence.

Election of Officers; Report of the Treasurer.

Discussions on "Whispering and Intercommunication among Scholars." by Messrs. Cady, Foster, Smith, Willard. Perry, and Leach; "Means for Securing Attention in School," by Messrs. Gamwell, Foster, Ladd, Mowry, and DeMunn; "The Influence of Education upon the Community," by Messrs. A. H. Clapp, J. B. Chapin, Sears, Stone, and Leach; "Written Examinations," by Messrs. Manchester, DeMunn, and Snow.

Remarks on "Means of Securing Punctual and Regular Attendance at School," by A. W. Godding.

The *Rhode Island Schoolmaster* was made the organ of the Institute, and a Board of Editors appointed, after discussion by Messrs. Mowry, Ladd, Foster, Snow, Godding, Robbins, Perry, Stone, Kent, Pierce, and Gamwell.

Statement of "The Progress of Education in Rhode Island, and the Work of the Institute," by E. M. Stone.

Resolutions of sympathy in the loss by death of John J. Stinson and Dana P. Colburn.

Fifty-fifth Meeting.—September 7th and 8th, 1860, at Bristol.

Lectures on "Obstacles in the Way of Intellectual Progress," by Dr. Chapin; "Normal Schools, their Origin, History, Claims and Results," by Rev. B. G. Northrop; "Means of Obtaining a Knowledge of the English Language," by J. Kendall; "Vivacity in the Teacher," by D. Goodwin; "Physical Training," by Dr. D. Lewis.

Discussions on "Too Great Attention to Arithmetic in our Schools," by Messss. Cady, Kendall, DeMunn, Snow, Robbins, Manchester, and Ladd; "The Subjects of the Lectures," by Messrs. Mowry, Pierce. Northrup, Ladd, DeMunn, Kendall, Chase. Mathewson, and Gallup; "The Interests of the *Rhode Island Schoolmaster*," by Messrs. DeMunn, Mowry, Cady. Kendall, and Willard.

Fifty-sixth Meeting.—October 12th, 1860, at East Greenwich.

Lectures by Messrs. J. M. Talbot, J. Kendall, and Dr. Lewis.

Fifty-seventh Meeting.—December 7th, 1860, at Blackstone. ·

Lectures by Messrs. S. S. Greene, H. K. Oliver, and W. A. Mowry.

Fifty-eighth Meeting.—January 18th and 19th, 1861, at Centreville.

Lecture on "Education," by Rev A. Gardiner.

Discussions on "Teaching Arithmetic: its Defects, and the Better Way," by Messrs. DeMunn, Kendall, and Manchester; "Education of Young Children," by J. Kendall; "Usefulness of Public Examinations," by Messrs. DeMunn, Manchester, Ladd, Willard, Snow, Kistler, Spaulding, and Kendall.

Fifty-ninth Meeting.—SEVENTEENTH ANNUAL MEETING.—January 25th and 26th, 1861, at Providence.

Report of the Treasurer; Election of Officers and of Board of Editors for the *Rhode Island Schoolmaster.*

Lectures on "The Relation of Mental Philosophy to Education," by B. G. Northrup; "The Sea," by Rev. L. Swain.

Discussion on "The Mechanical Performance of Arithmetical Operations," by Messrs. Willard, Stone, Leach, Green, Mowry, Ladd, Eastman, Pierce, Snow, Manchester, DeMunn, Austin, and Kendall.

Sixtieth Meeting.—March 1st and 2d, 1861, at South Kingstown.

Lectures on "Unwritten History," by Rev. A. Woodbury; "Writing," by S. A. Potter.

Discussions on "Means of Securing Punctual and Constant Attendance at School," by Messrs. Gardiner, Tefft, Patten, DeMunn, and Phelps; "Reading," by Messrs. Grosvenor, Briggs, Thurber, Leach, Potter, DeMunn, Snow, Tefft, Gardiner, and Tucker; "The Best Method of Teaching Arithmetic," by Messrs. Tefft, Snow, and DeMunn.

Sixty-first Meeting.—November 22d and 23d, 1861, at Carolina Mills.

Lectures on "Education," by H. Rousmaniere; "The Most Important Requisite in Teaching," by J. J. Ladd; "Class Recitations," by J. Kendall.

Discussion on "The Present Duties of Teachers to their Country," by Messrs. Greene, Stanton, Cady, Tillinghast, Kendall, Tefft, Seamans, Bailey, DeMunn, and Ladd.

Resolved, That contributions of one cent from each scholar be solicited, for the aid of wounded soldiers.

Sixty-second Meeting.—December 20th and 21st, 1861, at Peacedale.

Lectures on "The Relation of the Mind to the Body," by H. Rousmaniere; "Teaching Letters and Spelling," by J. Kendall.

Discussions on "Guarding Children Against Temptation, or Teaching Them to Resist It," by Messrs. Tefft, Maryot, M. S. Greene, Rousmaniere, Miller, Gorton, Clark, and Coon; "Difficulties in Teaching Geography," by Messrs. Tefft, Greene, Tillinghast, Stanton, and others; "Method of Illustrating Decimal Fractions," by Messrs. Tefft, Davis, Stanton, Tillinghast, Peckham, Bentley, Greene, and others; "Good Order in Schools," by Messrs. Mowry, Stanton, Briggs, Tillinghast, Kenneth, and Coon; "Recitations in Reading," by Messrs. Thurber, Davis, Tefft, Briggs, Miner, and Coon; "Securing Prompt Attendance at School," by Messrs. Clark, Kendall, Stanton, and Mowry.

Remarks on "The Duty of Teachers to their Country," by W. A. Mowry.

Sixty-third Meeting.—January 4th and 5th, 1862, at Chepachet.

Lectures on "Principles of True Education, and the Difficulties Which Oppose It," by H. Rousmaniere; "Arithmetic and its Abbreviations," by N. W. DeMunn; "Book-Keeping in Common Schools," by S. A. Potter.

Discussions on "The Best Method of Teaching Writing and Spelling," "The Connection of Oral and Written Arithmetic," "How Far English Composition Should be Taught," by Messrs. Rousmaniere, Chase, Brown, Peckham, Mowry, and others; "The Control of Teachers over their Pupils out of School."

Sixty-fourth Meeting.—EIGHTEENTH ANNUAL MEETING.—January 31st and February 1st, 1862, at Providence.

Reports of Treasurer and Recording Secretary; Election of Officers.

Lectures on "The Comforts and Pleasures of School-keeping," by Rev. L. Whiting; "Culture of the Voice," by S. Monroe, "English History," by G. Palmer.

Discussion on "Good Discipline in School and How Maintained," by Messrs. Willard, Cady, Mowry, Ladd. G. T. Day, and J. M. Talcott.

Recitations in "Arithmetic," conducted by N. W. DeMunn; in "English Grammar," conducted by A. J. Manchester

Appointment of a permanent committee to conduct the publication of the *Rhode Island Schoolmaster.*

Resolution, moved by E. M. Stone, recommending an increase of evening schools.

Sixty-fifth Meeting.—February 28th and March 1st, 1862, at Centreville, (Warwick.)

Lectures on "Writing," by S. A. Potter; "The Comforts and Pleasures of School-keeping," by L. Whiting, "Spelling," by J. Kendall; "The Study of the U. S. Constitution in our Schools," by W. A. Mowry.

Discussion on "The Teacher's Sphere of Usefulness," by Messrs. Husted, Leader, Brayton, and Cooke.

Recitations in "English History," conducted by D. R. Adams; "The Art of Map-drawing," conducted by S. A. Briggs.

Sixty-sixth Meeting.—April 11th and 12th, 1862, at Wickford.

Lecture on "The Teacher; his Works, and his Rewards," by A. J. Manchester.

Discussions on "The Defects in Our Public Schools," by Messrs. Allen, Chadsey, Slocum, Potter, and others; "The Relative Duties of Parents, Teachers, and Pupils," by Messrs. Ladd, and DeMunn; "Reading," by Messrs Manchester and DeMunn; 'The Present Duties of Teachers to their Country," by Messrs. Snow, Slocum, and others.

Remarks on "Penmanship," by S. A. Potter.

Exercises in "Reading," conducted by F. B. Snow.

Sixty seventh Meeting.—November 21st and 22d, 1862, at Westerly.

Lectures on "The Qualifications of the Teacher," by J. Kendall; "Education Out of School," by Rev. H. Lincoln.

Discussions on "The Responsibility of Teachers for the Punctuality and Attendance of Scholars," by Messrs. Kendall, Foster, Griswold, Woodbridge, Tefft, Greene, and Whitman; "Means of Making Rhode Island Pupils Fair Spellers," by Messrs. Kendall, Griswold, and Greene; "Educating a Community to a Right Appreciation of Good Teachers and Schools," by Messrs. Tefft, Foster, and Greene; "The Best Method of Presenting Decimals and Percentage," by Messrs. DeMunn, Kendall, Foster, Ladd, Greene, and others; "Elevating the Standard of Schools, and Exciting Pupils to Greater Diligence," by Messrs. Kendall, and Kenyon.

Sixty-eighth Meeting.—December 5th and 6th, 1862, at Wickford.

Lectures on "Object Lessons," by J. Kendall; "Nature's Hieroglyphs," by Rev. C. H. Fay.

Discussions on "The Dependence of Teachers upon Text-Books;" "The Responsibility of Teachers for the Lack of a Delicate Moral Tone in their Pupils," by Messrs. Snow, Kendall, and others.

Sixty-ninth Meeting.—December 19th and 20th, 1862, at Pawtucket.

Lectures on "The Progress of Public Schools," by Rev. G. Taft; "Book-keeping," by S. A. Potter; "The Duties of Parent Citizens to their Public Schools," by H. Rousmaniere; "The Scholar and his Country," by Rt. Rev. T. M. Clark.

Poem on "Nature and its Revelations," by W. M. Rodman.

Class exercises in "Spelling," conducted by J. Kendall, with remarks by Messrs. Snow, Willard, DeMunn, and others; "Reading," conducted by F. B. Snow.

Discussion on "The Moral Influence of Teachers upon their Pupils in and out of School," by Messrs. Willard, Mowry, Gamwell, Ladd, and others.

Seventieth Meeting.—January 9th and 10th, 1863, at Newtown, (Portsmouth.)

Lectures on "The Benefits of School Libraries," by Rev. S. D. Coggeshall; "The True Relation of School and Home, Teacher and Parent," by T. W. Bicknell; "The Cultivation of a Taste for the Beauties of Nature," by I. F. Cady.

Discussions on "School Libraries," by Messrs. Kendall, Rousmaniere, Coggeshall, and Arnold; "The Assignment of Lessons to be Studied at Home," by Messrs. Kendall, Arnold, Gifford, and others; "Preventing Whispering and Motion of the Lips while Studying," by S. D. Coggeshall; "The Importance of the Coöperation of Parents," by Messrs. Rousmaniere, Cady, Belden, and Kendall; "The Assumption of Unwarranted Authority by Teachers," by Messrs. Bicknell, Cady, and Belden; "Method of Commencing the Study of Geography," by Messrs. Cady, Kendall, Chapman, and others.

Seventy-first Meeting.—NINETEENTH ANNUAL MEETING.—January 30th and 31st, 1863, at Providence.

Report of the Treasurer; total amount of funds, $1,237 61; Election of Officers.

Lectures on "English Grammar," by Prof. S. S. Greene; "The Importance and Mode of Training the Senses," by Rev. B. G. Northrup; "Physical Geography," by B. Harrison.

Discussions on "The Responsibility of the Teacher for the Moral Conduct of His Pupils," by Messrs. Cady, and DeMunn; "English Grammar," by Messrs. Cady, Willard, Tefft, Belden, Manchester, DeMunn, and Northrup; "The necessity of Sustaining the *Rhode Island Schoolmaster*," by Messrs. Matteson, Northrup and Ladd.

Class exercises in "Object Teaching," conducted by N. A. Calkins; "Spelling and Reading," by a class of colored children.

8

Messrs. Ladd and DeMunn appointed to memorialize the legislature for an act of incorporation.

Seventy-second Meeting.—February 19th and 20th, 1863, at Ashaway.

Lectures on "The Teacher and His Work," by J. J. Ladd; "The Duties of Parents and the Public in Regard to Schools," by H. Rousmaniere; "School Tactics," by J. Kendall.

Discussions on "Methods of Securing Greater Punctuality in Schools," by Messrs. Langworthy, Saunders, Greene, Kenneth, Maryott, Davis, Ladd, Collins, Stanton, Vincent, Morton, Coon, Rev. J. Clark, Rev. H. Clark, and Lewis; "The Use of Text-Books in Recitations," by Messrs. Ladd and Kendall.

Class exercise in "Bassini's Method of Teaching Music," conducted by J. M. Stillman.

Seventy-third Meeting.—March 6th and 7th, 1863, at Kingston.

Lectures on "The Scale on which the Universe is Built," by J. Kendall; "Mental Science," by H. Rousmaniere.

Poem on "The Golden Era," by A. J. Foster.

Discussion on the use of Text-Books in Recitations," by Messrs. Kendall, Eastman, Greene, Rousmaniere, Tefft, and others.

Seventy-fourth Meeting.—————, at River Point.

Lectures on "English Grammar," by A. A. Gamwell; "————," by Rev. J. M. H. Dow.

Discussions on "The Best Method of Teaching Geography," by Messrs. Rousmaniere, Aldrich, Fuller, Harrison, Seamans, Eldridge, and Gallup; "The Most Prominent Faults in our Common Schools," by Messrs. Rousmaniere, Matteson, Eastman, Willard, Gamwell, Spaulding, and Kent.

Remarks on "Penmanship," by B. Harrison.

Seventy-fifth Meeting.—November 24th and 25th, 1863, at Westerly.

Lectures on "The Study of the English Language," by W. A. Mowry; "Duties of Parents to the School," by Dr. J. B. Chapin; "Entrance to the Public High Schools Should be Determined by Scholarship, Ascertained by Competitive Examination," by Hon. H. Barnard.

Discussions on "The Extent to which Teachers Should Assist their Pupils," by Messrs. Foster, Greene, Mowry, Chapin, and others; "The Greatest Evil in our Schools, and its Remedy," by Messrs. Ladd, Ames, Mowry, and others.

School Reports were given by Messrs. Greene, Woodbridge, Coon, Tillinghast, Inman, Collins, Foster, Kenyon, Robbins and Mowry.

Exercises in Gymnastics, by Messrs. Trine and Wood.

Seventy-sixth Meeting.—December 11th and 12th, 1863, at North Scituate.

Lectures on "The Good Teacher," by Rev. Lyman Whiting; "Vitality in the School-room," by John J. Ladd.

Discussions on "The Extent and Mode of the Teacher's Help to His Pupils in Mathematics," "The Use of the Blackboard in English Grammar,"

" Methods of Teaching Spelling," " Proper and Improper Penalties for Defective Recitations, or Bad Conduct," " Topical Recitations."

Seventy-seventh Meeting.—January 15th and 16th, 1874, at Centreville.

Lectures on " The Obstacles in the way of Successful Teaching." by J. B. Chapin; " The Teacher's Motives and Difficulties," by A. J. Manchester.

Discussions on " The Schools of Rhode Island Compared with those of Twenty Years Ago," by Messrs. Rousmaniere, Husted, Adams, Seamans, Stone, and Matteson; "The Teaching of Music in our Schools," by Messrs Rousmaniere, Gallup, Matteson, Ladd, Spencer, Berry, and Kent; " The Obstacles to the Success of our Schools," by Messrs. Ladd, Spaulding, Rousmaniere, and Mowry.

Reports from Schools, by Messrs. Kent, Berry, Gallup, Bates, Manchester, Edwards, Eastman, Tefft, Robbins, Spaulding and Mowry.

Exercises in Gymnastics, by Dr. Wood.

Remarks eulogistic of the lamented D. P. Colbourn, by Messrs. Ladd Mowry, and Austin.

Seventy-eighth Meeting.—TWENTIETH ANNUAL MEETING.—January 29th, and 30th, 1864, at Providence.

Election of Officers.

Lectures on " Morning Glories," by J. Kendall; " Object Teaching," by I. F. Cady; " The Study of History," by Rev. B. Sears; " The Relation of the Scholar to the Rebellion," by J. T. Edwards; "Self Education." by J. D. Philbrick; " Physical Geography," by Prof. S. Tenney; " The Relations of Parents to the School," by T. W. Bicknell.

Report on the history and conduct of the *Rhode Island Schoolmaster* during the year, by N. W. DeMunn.

Seventy-ninth Meeting—February 12th and 13th, 1864, at Woonsocket.

Lectures on " Familiar Topics," by J. Kendall; " Supervision of School," by Rev. B. S. Northrup; " Relation of the Scholar to the Rebellion," by J. T. Edwards; " Education and Physical Interests," by Hon. J. B. Chapin.

Discussions on " Parental Interest in Schools," "Object Teaching as a System," " Physical Culture," " Defects in Public Schools."

Eightieth Meeting.—June 3d and 4th, 1864, at Harrisville.

Lectures on " The Education of the Freedmen," by Rev. A. Root; " Reading." by F. B. Snow; " Primary Geography," by T. W. Bicknell; " The Educational Improvements of Twenty-five Years," by I. F. Cady.

Discussions on " The Best Means of Securing Regular Attendance at School by Messrs. Steere, Metcalf, and Webb; " The Evils of a Frequent Change of Teachers, and the Remedy." by Messrs. Cady, Bicknell, and Mowry; " Method of Teaching Writing in Common Schools." by Messrs. Webb, Steere, and others; " Teaching Beginners in Arithmetic the Process Before the Reasoning," by Messrs. Snow, and Mowry; " Requiring Pupils to give Information of Offenses," by Messrs. Mowry, Cady, Webb, Steere, and others.

Eighty-first Meeting.—Phenix, October 7th and 8th, 1864.

The Institute held the first of its series of meetings for the season in this village.

The question, "At What Age Should Children Commence Taking Writing Lessons, and When Should They Begin the Study of Geography and Grammar?" was discussed by Hon. Henry Rousmaniere, Rev. B. P. Byram, Messrs. Kent, Seamans, and Spaulding.

Class exercise in Spelling, conducted by Mr. J. R. Kent.

"Ought Parents to be Compelled to send their Children to School?" discussed by Hon Henry Rousmaniere, Rev. Charles H. Titus, Rev. B. P. Byram, and Messrs. Seamans, and Spaulding.

Evening session.—Mr. Harris R. Greene, Principal of the Worcester, Mass., High School, delivered a lecture "On the Moral Influence of the Teacher in the School Room."

Saturday morning.—Mr. A. A. Gamwell, of Providence, presented the following subject, "How to Teach Pupils the Use of the English Language, and its History as the Work of Man;" lecture, "Strike while the Iron is Hot," by Rev. James T. Edwards.

Afternoon session.—The question, "What are the Most Apparent Hindrances to the Elevation of Public Schools?" was discussed by Hon. Henry Rousmaniere, Rev. J. T. Edwards, the President, and N. W. DeMunn. The customary vote of thanks to lecturers, and for hospitality, were passed. Adjourned.

Eighty-second Meeting.—East Greenwich, October 21st and 22d, 1854. A large assembly met in the Seminary Chapel. Remarks, by the President, William A. Mowry The first subject presented was, "What are Mile Stones Marking Educational Progress?" discussed by Hon. Henry Rousmaniere, Rev. J. T. Edwards, Professor J. Eastman, Rev. S. A. Crane, D. D., and Dr. Eldredge; second topic, "What Studies Demand More Attention in our Public Schools than they now Receive?' discussed by the President, Rev. Messrs. Edwards, and Crane, and Commissioner Chapin. Singing, by a class of ladies and gentlemen under the direction of Professor Tourjee.

Evening session.—The second topic of the afternoon was further discussed. Rev. J. H. McCarty delivered a lecture upon "The Lights and Shadows of the School Room. Professor Tourjee, with his class, sang a portion of Rossini's "Stabat Mater," with fine effect.

Saturday morning.—Business.—Commissioner Chapin urged the importance of establishing on a firmer basis a State Normal School. A committee of one from each county was appointed to prepare a set of questions for discussion at the coming Institutes, and report the same at the next meeting. The question, "What Considerations are Sufficient to Warrant a Change in Text-Books?" was discussed by Messrs. Kendall, Chapin, DeMunn, and Edwards.

Afternoon session.—Questions were answered relative to "Correcting whispering, loud study, tardiness," etc. The claims of the *Rhode Island*

Schoolmaster were urged by Mr. DeMunn. Thirty-two subscriptions were obtained. The customary resolutions of thanks were passed, and after a song by Professor Tourjee's music class, the Institute adjourned. The members were received on the Seminary grounds by the "Seminary Guards," and escorted to the depot.

Eighty-third Meeting.—East Providence, November 18th and 19th, 1864. Hon. Joshua B. Chapin, Commissioner of Public Schools, delivered a discourse on "The True Teacher," several points of which were discussed by President Mowry, and Rev. G. M. P King

Evening session.—"The Importance of the Coöperation of Parents with Teachers, and the Best Method of Securing It," was discussed by Messrs. Mowry, King, and others. Rev. Leonard Swain, D. D., of Providence, delivered a lecture upon "Puritan Education."

Saturday morning.—"English Grammar in Connection with Analysis," was presented by Mr. Francis B. Snow, and discussed by Messrs. Barney, Mowry, Kendall, Cady, Chapin, Gamwell, and others; "Lessons from Nature," was a topic considered by Mr. I. F. Cady.

Afternoon session.—The importance of parental coöperation was further discussed. Mr. Joshua Kendall read a paper on "Difficulties Arising in the School Room." The committee appointed at the last meeting of the Institute to prepare a series of questions for discussion, reported. These questions embraced a consideration of the utility of the Normal School, more uniform and more thorough examinations, the modification required in the school laws, what will authorize establishing a Grammar or High School in the country towns. It was also announced that a meeting of School Committees, Trustees, Superintendents, and others, for mutual consultation would be held in Providence at the next annual meeting. After passing resolutions of thanks, the Institute adjourned.

Eighty-fourth Meeting.—TWENTY-FIRST ANNUAL MEETING.—Providence, January 27th and 28th, 1865.

The annual meeting of the Institute was held in the vestry of the Richmond Street Church.

Election of Officers.

The meeting was opened with devotional exercises by Rev. Mr. Richardson, pastor of the church. The President, Mr. Mowry, made an address of welcome to the teachers. Various committees were appointed. Professor J. Eastman, of the Providence Conference Seminary, gave a lecture upon "Duties of the Teacher to Himself."

Afternoon session.—The State Commissioner, in behalf of a committee appointed to memorialize the General Assembly for an appropriation to establish an "Experimental School" in "Object Teaching," reported that they had attended to the duty assigned them, but without being able to effect anything in accordance with the resolution. Lecture, "English Composition," by Rev. S. A. Crane, D. D., of East Greenwich. Address on the same subject by Professor Robinson P. Dunn, of Brown University.

Evening session.—Music, by the "Orpheus Club." Lecture by Rev. E. B. Webb, of Boston; subject, "Given, a Man—How to Make the Most of Him"

Saturday morning.—Mr. N. W. DeMunn reported in relation to the *Rhode Island Schoolmaster.* Lecture by E. A. Sheldon, Esq, Superintendent of Schools at Oswego, N. Y., on "Child Culture by the Methods of Object Teaching."

Editors of the *Rhode Island Schoolmaster* for the ensuing year were elected. Lecture on "Ventilation," by D. B. Thayer, Esq., of Jamaica Plains, Mass.

Afternoon session.—Lecture on "History," by Rev. Barnas Sears, D. D., of Brown University. Resolutions of thanks to the several lecturers, the "Orpheus Club," the Richmond street society, and the several railroads for free return tickets to teachers and other friends of education passing over them, were passed. Also a resolution of thanks and good wishes to Mr. Joshua Kendall, who had resigned the Principalship of the State Normal School. Adjourned.

Eighty-fifth Meeting.—Newtown, (Portsmouth), December 22d and 23d, 1865.

The Institute met at Masonic Hall. It was expected that Commissioner Chapin would deliver a lecture on Thursday evening, but owing to a severe storm, he was unable to reach the island. In place of the lecture the "Eight Hour System of Labor," was discussed.

Friday morning—"Arithmetic and the Principles of Substraction," were discussed. In the afternoon, "The Best Methods of Teaching Grammar" were discussed, by Messrs. Mowry, Baggs, Inman, and Bicknell. In the evening Mr. Bicknell, Principal of the Arnold Street Grammar School, Providence, read a lecture on "The Teacher's Compensation," President Mowry spoke of "The Relations of the School to the State, and the Duties of Parents, School Officers, and Friends of Education in Elevating the Standard of our Public Schools."

Saturday morning.—"School Discipline," was discussed by Messrs. Morse, Thomas and Mowry. Mr. Albert J. Manchester, of Providence, gave a lecture upon "The Teacher, His Works and Rewards." Mr. S. A. Potter, author of Potter & Hammond's series of writing books, explained the principles of his system of penmanship, giving illustrations on the blackboard. Adjourned.

Eighty-sixth Meeting.—Lonsdale, December 29th and 30th, 1865.

The Institute met in the High School room. "School Discipline" was discussed by Messrs. Chapin, Mowry, Lansing, and Ross. The evening session was held in the Sunday School room of Christ Church. A lecture on "The Sensibilities" was delivered by Rev. B. G. Northrup, of Saxonville, Mass. Erastus Richardson, Esq., of Woonsocket, read a racy poem on "The Gift of Speech."

Saturday morning.—A lecture on "Grammar" was given by Mr. A. Gamwell, of Providence. The subject of the *Rhode Island Schoolmaster* was presented, and a large number of subscriptions obtained. Resolutions of thanks were passed, and the Institute adjourned.

Eighty-sixth Meeting.—TWENTY-SECOND ANNUAL MEETING.—Providence, January 26th and 27th, 1866.

Election of Officers.

The Institute met in the vestry of the Central Congregational Church, and a hearty address of welcome was made by Rev. Leonard Swain, D. D. Various committees were appointed. Professor Robinson P. Dunn, of Brown University, delivered a lecture upon "The Study of English Literature."

Afternoon session.—A lecture by Professor Samuel S. Greene, of Brown University, "Teaching as an Answer to the Internal Want of the Pupil." A lecture by Professor J. Lewis Diman, of Brown University, on "Political Education in Public Schools." President Sears spoke briefly in support of the views presented in the lecture.

Evening session.—Lecture on "The Educational Mission at the South," by Colonel T. W. Higginson, of Newport.

Saturday morning.—Resolutions were introduced by Professor Dunn, and unanimously adopted, in grateful recognition of the important services to the cause of education, rendered by the late Rev. Francis Wayland, D. D., LL. D. S. H. Taylor, LL. D., of Phillips Academy, Andover, Mass., gave a colloquial lecture upon the "Topography of Rome."

Afternoon session.—The Board of Editors of the *Rhode Island Schoolmaster* was elected. Professor Josiah P. Cooke, Jr., of Harvard University, delivered a lecture upon "The Value of Scientific Studies as a Means of Discipline." The interests of the *Schoolmaster* were presented. Resolutions of congratulation and also of thanks were presented and adopted. Likewise resolutions of gratitude upon the return of peace and the altered condition of the country. A short closing address was made by President Bicknell, and the Institute adjourned.

Eighty-seventh Meeting.—Peacedale. February 15th and 16th, 1866, afternoon session.

The Institute met in Hazard's Hall, and was cordially welcomed by Rev. M. Williams. The subject, "Ought Parents to Visit Schools?" was discussed by Messrs. Bicknell, Aldrich, Tefft, Collins, and Williams. A discussion followed on "Whispering in School," which was participated in by the President, and Messrs. Hazard, Williams, Richmond, Tefft, Collins, and Aldrich.

Evening session.—Lectures were delivered on "The Legend of Rocks," by Mr. M. A. Aldrich, of Providence; on "School Morale," by Mr. Francis B. Snow, of Providence; on "Moral, Physical and Intellectual Culture," by Hon. Rowland G. Hazard, of Peacedale.

Saturday morning.—"School Morale" was discussed by Messrs. DeMunn, and Williams. A lecture was read by Mr. F. B. Snow, on "Reading," and another, by Mr. N. W. DeMunn, on "Some of the Best

Methods of Teaching Arithmetic." Remarks on the same subject were made by Mr. Hazard. Resolutions of thanks to lecturers, and also for hospitable entertainment, were passed. Adjourned.

Eighty-eighth Meeting.—Newport, March 1st, 2d and 3d, 1866.

The Institute temporarily organized on Thursday evening, and Commissioner Chapin delivered a lecture on "Education, its Importance and Results."

Friday morning.—An address of welcome was given by Rev. Charles II. Malcom, to which President Bicknell responded. Rev. Cyrus II. Fay, of Providence, delivered a lecture upon "Some of the Evils of our System of Instruction."

Afternoon session.—Mr. S. A. Potter, of Providence, delivered an address on "Moral Instruction in Schools." A resolution declaring it to be "the duty of those in authority to shorten the daily sessions of the Public Schools," was, after discussion, adopted. Mr. F. B. Snow, of Providence, read a lecture on "Moral Instruction in Schools; How to Teach It, and When to Teach It."

Evening session.—Lecture by Rev. S. Reed, of Providence, on "What I Saw in a Nine Miles Walk in the Mammoth Cave."

Saturday morning.—Discussion, "The Necessity and Means of Interesting the Pupil," participated in by Messrs. Higginson, White, Talbot, Ladd, and Snow. Lecture by Professor Samuel S. Greene, of Brown University, upon "Teaching as Satisfying an Internal Want of the Pupil," Mr. John J. Ladd gave a familiar talk on "School Discipline." The claims of the *Rhode Island Schoolmaster* were presented. Resolutions of thanks for the hospitality extended to the members of the Institute were passed; also, to the several lecturers, to the railroad companies, and to the American Steamboat Company, for special favors received. Adjourned.

Eighty-ninth Meeting.—Pawtucket, October 10th, 11th and 12th, 1866.

The Institute met in the lecture room of the Methodist Episcopal Church. Words of welcome were spoken by Rev. Mr. Church, and replied to by the President.

Dr. Lowell Mason gave a lecture on "The Best Methods of Teaching the Art of Vocal Music." Prof. F. S. Jewell, of the State Normal School, at Albany, N. Y., gave a class exercise in Spelling. Dr. Chapin closed the exercises of the morning with a few pertinent remarks on the lecture.

Wednesday afternoon.—Class exercise on "Writing," by Mr. Bowler. Class exercise in "Arithmetic," conducted by Mr. J. F. Claflin, Principal of the High School in Worcester, Mass. Colloquial lecture on "Grammar and Analysis," by Professor Jewell. Lecture on "The True Uses of History," by President Sears of Brown University.

Thursday morning.—Exercise on "Vocal Music," by Dr. Mason. A paper on "Declamation," by Mr. Claflin. Class exercise in "Geography," by Professor Jewell.

Afternoon session.—Second exercise on "Writing," by Mr. Bowler.

Exercises on "Reading," and on "Fractions," by Mr. G. N. Bigelow. Lecture on "Geometry," by Professor S. S. Greene.

Evening session.—Lecture on "Temperance," by Dr. Charles Jewett, of Worcester, Mass.

Friday morning.—Lecture on "The Principles and Uses of Music," by Dr. Mason. Lesson in "Notation," by Mr. Bigelow. Essay on "Health," by Dr. Trine, of Providence.

Afternoon session.—"Grammar and Analysis," by Professor Jewell. "Elocution," by Professor Mark Bailey, of Yale College. Resolutions in favor of a State Normal School, and of Normal Institutes, to be sustained by a State appropriation, were adopted; also the customary resolutions of thanks.

Friday evening.—Lecture on "Normal Schools," by Professor Jewell. A committee on "The Normal School," consisting of two gentlemen from each county in the State, was appointed to act in connection with the committee appointed by the Board of Directors of the Institute. After a few appropriate remarks by the President, the singing of "America," by the audience, and a benediction, by Professor Jewell, the Institute adjourned.

Ninetieth Meeting.—TWENTY-THIRD ANNUAL MEETING.—Providence, January 26th, 1867.

Election of officers.

The Institute convened at the school-rooms of Messrs. Mowry & Goff.

The President, in his opening remarks, alluded to the unusual nature of the annual meeting for this year, and called the attention of the Institute to the several topics to be discussed and acted upon by them. Chief among these subjects were the true office and proper field of action of the Institute, the reëstablishment of the Normal School, and the evils of truancy.

On motion of Commissioner Chapin, it was

Voted, That a committee to consist of two from each county in the State, and six members of the Institute, be appointed to consider the question of the reëstablishment of the Normal School, and to memorialize the General Assembly on the subject; and that the Mayor and the Superintendent of Public Schools in Providence, and such other persons as the School Committee of said city shall be pleased to appoint, be respectfully requested to coöperate with the above committee.

It was also voted that a committee of three be appointed to memorialize the General Assembly to make an appropriation of five hundred dollars for the purpose of maintaining two Institutes of Instruction of one week each in length, in different parts of the State, during each year, under the supervision of the School Commissioner. The same committee was also empowered to memorialize the General Assembly on the subject of "Truancy." *

---

* The committee on re-establishing the Normal School were, Rev. John Boyden, Woonsocket; Hon. T. R. King, Pawtucket; Professor George W. Greene, East

The resident and contributing editors of the *Rhode Island Schoolmaster* were appointed for the ensuing year, and a motion to appoint a committee of three " to consider any proposition that may be made for merging the *Schoolmaster* into a New England Educational Journal, and report on the same to the Institute," was, after free discussion, laid on the table. A motion to put forth every endeavor to increase the circulation of the *Schoolmaster*, was adopted.

Resolutions were unanimously passed in favor of establishing a " National Bureau of Education " at Washington, accompanied with a request to the Senators in the United States Congress from Rhode Island, that they endeavor to secure the passage of a bill providing for such a Bureau. The thanks of the Institute were tendered to Messrs. Mowry & Goff, for the use of their rooms. Adjourned.

Ninety-first Meeting.—TWENTY-FOURTH ANNUAL MEETING.—Providence, January 24th and 25th, 1868.

Election of Officers.

The Institute met in the vestry of the Central Congregational Church. Devotional exercises and address of welcome by Rev. Mr. Vose. Response by President Bicknell. The usual committees were appointed. Lecture on " Educational Wants," by Thomas L. Angell, A. M., Principal of the Lapham Institute.

Afternoon session.—Lectures " How to Teach Children," by Professor Samuel S. Greene, of Brown University; " Elocution," by Colonel II. B. Sprague, of the Connecticut State Normal School; "Symmetrical Culture," by Rev. James T. Edwards, East Greenwich.

Evening session.—Lecture by Colonel II. B. Sprague, on " Milton as a Teacher." A large and gratified audience was in attendance.

Saturday morning.—Address on "The Educational System of Great Britain," by Hon. Neal Dow, of Portland, Maine. Lectures, "On the Metrical System," by Professor J. II. Appleton, of Brown University; " Relations of the Teacher and Pupil," by J. II. Tenney, Esq., of Newton Centre, Mass. Exercise in " Geography," by Mrs. Mary R. C. Smith, of Oswego, N. Y. The resident and monthly editors of the *Schoolmaster* were appointed. Resolutions in favor of more frequent meetings of the Institute in different parts of the State; in commendation of the *Schoolmaster*; in appreciation of the services of the retiring President; in favor of reëstablishing the Normal School; and of thanks to lecturers, and for various courtesies, were passed. The following resolution was also unanimously adopted:

Greenwich; Hon. B. Lapham, Warwick; Hon. Elisha R. Potter, Kingston; Hon. R. G. Hazard, Peace Dale; W. A. White, Esq., and B. H. Rhodes, Esq., of Newport; Rev. Thomas Shepard, D. D., Bristol; Mr. Isaac F. Cady, Warren.

Committee on the Institute and on Tenney, Thomas W. Bicknell, Barrington; Rev. Barnas Sears. D. D., John Kingsbury, LL. D., and Samuel Austin, Providence; William A. Mowry, Cranston; Rev. James T. Edwards. East Greenwich.

Resolved, That in the death of Rev. Robinson P. Dunn, D. D., Professor of Rhetoric and English Literature in Brown University, the Institute sincerely mourns the loss of a member whose Christian character, ripe scholarship, and earnest interest in the cause of popular education, greatly endeared him to a wide circle of friends.

Adjourned.

Ninety-second Meeting.—Wakefield, February 28th and 29th, 1868.

Discussion, "The Teacher's Daily Preparation for the Duties of the School-room;" participated in by Rev. Mr. Wheeler, and Messrs. De-Munn, Aldrich, and others.

Evening session.—Lecture by Rev. James T. Edwards, of East Greenwich Seminary, on "The Use and Abuse of Illustrations."

Saturday morning.—"The Proper Method of Teaching Geography," by President DeMunn. The "Study of Grammar," by Mr. M. A. Aldrich. "Arithmetic, with Special Reference to Square Root," by the President. Hon. Elisha R. Potter, described the working of the system of common schools in the State. The "rate bill system" was operating injuriously on many districts. Resolutions in favor of local meetings of the Institute, and in behalf of the *Schoolmaster*, were adopted. Also the usual vote of thanks. Adjourned.

Ninety-third Meeting.—TWENTY-FIFTH ANNUAL MEETING.—January 29th and 30th, 1869, at Providence.

Election of Officers.

This session of the Institute was held in connection with one of the series of meetings conducted by the School Commissioner. A committee was appointed to confer with the committee on education in the General Assembly, in reference to a *Normal School*. A committee on the *Rhode Island Schoolmaster* was appointed with power to act.

Adjourned.

Ninety-fourth Meeting.—TWENTY-SIXTH ANNUAL MEETING.—Providence, January 29th and 30th, 1870.

Election of Officers.

The Institute met in Roger Williams Hall. Devotional exercises conducted at the opening by Rev. Thomas Laurie, D. D. Address of welcome to teachers by Rev. Augustus Woodbury, and responded to by President Edwards. Lecture by Professor James Johonnot, of Oswego, N. Y., on "The Philosophy of Teaching." Address, by Rev. B. G. Northrup, Secretary of Connecticut Board of Education, upon "The Laws of Massachusetts, Rhode Island and Connecticut, in Relation to Employing Children in Manufacturing Establishments."

Afternoon session.—The hall was filled to its utmost capacity. Various committees were announced. "Teaching History," an exercise conducted by Mr. Albert J. Manchester, Principal of the Thayer Street Grammar School assisted by a class of his pupils. Recitation, "The Black Regiment," by Master Willie Weeden, of the same school. Singing by two hundred pupils from the Grammar schools of Providence, under the direction of Mr. Henry Carter. Readings, by Miss LeRow, of Boston. A paper on "Teaching Primary Geography, by Means of Object Lessons," read by Mrs. Rebecca Jones, of Worcester, Mass., and illustrated with a class of children. Address, by Rev. B. G. Northrup.

Evening session.—The hall was crowded, and hundreds were unable to gain admission. Music, by the "Choral Union," of Pawtucket, and the choir of the First Baptist Church in Providence, under the direction of Mr. George W. Haselwood, assisted by Mr. C. W. Bradley. Address of welcome by His Excellency Governor Seth Padelford, who closed with the following words:

"I welcome you, ladies and gentlemen, to this city, to this hall, and to the hospitalities of the occasion. I hope that all your deliberations and discussions will prove conducive to the objects in view, and that by elevating the standard of education, and exciting a new interest for its diffusion, a fresh impulse will be given to the cause throughout the State. In this series of meetings you have my best wishes for their success, and I trust that the occasion will leave many pleasant reminiscences."*

Hon. George L. Clarke, Mayor of Providence, addressed the meeting with words of greeting. This overflowing audience, he said, he regarded as a good omen for the cause of education in this State. It is too late to ask whether our school system should be abandoned. Its benefits are settled beyond question. The questions now to be asked are, how can the system be improved? how can we reap greater success? how can the money appropriated secure its best results? The school system of Providence he regarded as not excelled in the United States, and perhaps not in the world. But it is not perfect while one child is allowed to grow up in ignorance—that parent of vice and crime. Alluding to Massachusetts, he said that Rhode Island cannot expect to hold her rank unless she spends more money and time in the development of her brain power. Rhode Island needs a Board of Education and a good Normal School, or she will be outstripped by every New England State, if not every State.

Spirited addresses were also made by President Edwards, Rev. Augustus Woodbury, Hon. B. G. Northrup, Henry Howard, Esq., and General Charles C. Van Zandt.

Saturday morning.—A resolution recommending the *Rhode Island Schoolmaster* " to the continued patronage and support of teachers and the friends of education at home and abroad," was adopted. Lecture, by Professor Johonnot, "On Subjective and Objective Teaching." Address by Hon. John Kingsbury. Lecture on "Reading," with illustra-

---

* Ex-Governor Padelford, as a member of the Common Council in Providence, from 1837 to 1841, and from 1851 to 1852, as also for fifteen years a member of the school committee, has rendered important services to the public schools. He actively coöperated with others in securing a High School for the city of Providence, and while Governor, bestowed upon the Normal School, and the schools of the State, very faithful attention.

tions, by Professor Lewis B. Munroe, of Boston. Singing, by two hundred pupils from the lower rooms of the Grammar schools of Providence, under the direction of Mrs. Mary E. Rawson.

Afternoon session.—Lecture " On the Principles of Teaching Geography, particularly in the department of Map Drawing," by Mr. J. M. Sawin, Principal of the Elm Street Grammar School, Providence, assisted by a class of his pupils.

Resolutions in favor of a Board of Education, and a Normal School, and of thanks to all who had in any way contributed to the profit or pleasure of the occasion, were passed. Readings, by Professor Munroe. After brief closing remarks by the President, followed by singing the Doxology, "Praise God," and a benediction by Rev. J. C. Stockbridge, D. D., the Institute adjourned.

Ninety-fifth Meeting.—September 22d, 23d, and 24th, 1870, at North Scituate.

Address of welcome, by Rev. O. H. True. Lecture on " Absenteeism From Our Schools," by Professor George W. Ricker. The subject was discussed by the Commissioner of Public Schools, and Messrs. True, Cole, Ellis, Saunders, and Fisher. Address on " The Prussian System of Education," by Rev. J. C. Stockbridge, D. D. A memorial to the General Assembly relating to a *Normal School*, was read by Dr. Fisher, and received a large number of signatures. The subject of " Ventilation," was presented by Rev. Daniel Leach, of Providence, and discussed by Dr. Fisher, and Prof. Ricker. Mr. Leach also presented the subject of " Spelling," in an interesting and instructive manner. Brief address by Governor Padelford. Reading from " The Trial of Pickwick," by Mr. F. G. Morley. Class exercise in " Arithmetic," by Mr. Albert J. Manchester. The claims of the *Rhode Island Schoolmaster* were presented. An exercise in " Reading " was given by Mr. F. B. Snow.

On the evening of the first day a popular meeting was held, and addresses were made by Governor Padelford, Rev. Daniel Leach, Albert J. Manchester, Commissioner Bicknell, Rev. O. H. True, Dr. C. H. Fisher, and Prof. G. H. Ricker. Adjourned.

Ninety-sixth Meeting.—December 15th and 16th, 1870, at Warren.

Address of welcome, by Rev. L. C. Manchester. Remarks, by Prof. F. S. Jewell, and Hon. Henry Barnard. Lecture "On English Grammar," by Mr Samuel Thurber, of Hyde Park, Mass. " Importance of Education," by J. W. Stillman. An exercise in " Spelling," with a class, conducted by Mrs. Smith, of the Meeting Street Colored School, Providence. An exercise in " English Grammar," by F. G. Morley. An Essay by Mr. Peck, of the Warren High School. Readings, by A. P. Mowry. An exercise in Arithmetic, by Mr. A. J. Manchester. Addresses and discussions by Prof. Jewell, Hon. Henry Barnard, General G. L. Cooke, and others.

Ninety-seventh Meeting.--TWENTY-SEVENTH ANNUAL MEETING —January 26th, 27th and 28th, 1871, at Providence.

Election of officers.

The first day was devoted by members of the Institute to visiting the
city schools for the purpose of witnessing the methods of study, instruc-
tion and recitation. In the evening the Institute met in Roger Williams
Hall, and listened to an address by Professor J. Lewis Diman, of Brown
University, on "Poetry in Education." Professor Hibbard, of Wesleyan
University, also gave select readings.

Friday morning.—An address of welcome was given by Hon. Thomas
A. Doyle, Mayor of Providence. The exercises of the day were "Disci-
pline," by O. H. Kile, A. M., of Westerly; Singing, by pupils of the
Thayer Street Grammar School, under the direction of Mr. B. W. Hood;
Lecture, by Professor George I. Chace, of Brown University; Select
Readings, by Prof. M. D. Brown, of Tufft's College; "Elements of Suc-
cess and Causes of Failure in Teaching," by Mr. F. W. Tilton, of New-
port. Remarks, by Hon. Joseph White, Secretary of Massachusetts
Board of Education; "Gymnastic Drill," by pupils of the Thayer Street
Grammar School.

In the evening the meeting was held in Harrington's Opera House.
Addresses by President Manchester, Hon. Thomas A. Doyle, Hon.
Joseph White, of Boston, and Hon. Warren Johnson, of Maine. Readings were given by Mrs. Miller, and Professor Brown. Music, under the
direction of Mr. Hood.

Saturday, at Roger Williams Hall.—Address on "Reading," by Professor Brown. "The Significance of Geographical Names," by Hon.
Joseph White. Remarks were made by Messrs. Leach, Johnson, White,
Perry, Tewksbury, and Waterman. A resolution to petition the General
Assembly to aid in elevating the standard of education in the State, by
establishing a Normal and Training School, was unanimously adopted.
A committee on the *Rhode Island Schoolmaster* was appointed; also, a
committee on the "State Teachers' Annual Excursion;" also, a committee to prepare a "Manual of the Rhode Island Institute of Instruction."
The customary resolutions of thanks were passed. The several sessions
of this Institute meeting were conducted with great spirit. The attendance was large, showing unabated interest to the close.

Ninety eighth Meeting.—TWENTY-EIGHTH ANNUAL MEETING.—January
18th, 19th and 20th, 1872, at Providence.

Election of Officers.

The first day (Thursday) was devoted to visiting the schools of the
city and the Normal School. In the evening a re-union of teachers was
held in Roger Williams Hall, at which music was given by the Brown
University Glee Club, and readings by Mrs. H. M. Miller.

Friday, at Roger Williams Hall.—A paper on "Practical Education,"
by A. D. Small, of Newport; Essay, by Mr. D. W. Hoyt, of the Providence High School; Music, by the pupils of the public schools in Providence, under the direction of Mr. B. W. Hood; Reading, by pupils from
the State Normal School; Essay, by J. C. Greenough, Principal of the
Normal School.

In the evening, at Music Hall.—Addresses, by Governor Padelford, Hon. Mayor Doyle, Hon. T. W. Bicknell, Rev. Daniel Leach, Rev. Alexis Caswell, D D., and Hon W. P. Sheffield. Readings, by Professor L. B. Monroe. Music, by pupils of the city public schools, and on the organ by Mr. F. F. Tingley.

Saturday morning, at Roger Williams Hall.—An annual tax of one dollar for gentlemen and fifty cents for ladies was voted. An exercise in Elocution was given by Professor Monroe, with the pupils of the Normal School. Messrs. Lyon, Bicknell, Hoyt, Greenough, and Small, were chosen a committee to publish the proceedings of this session of the Institute. A committee on the *Rhode Island Schoolmaster* was appointed. The death of Mr. Albert A. Gamwell was announced, and the following resolution unanimously adopted by a rising vote:

Resolved, That in the death of Mr. A. A. Gamwell, a Vice President of this Institute, and one of its earliest members, and for nearly twenty-five years a teacher in the city of Providence, this Institute and the cause of education have sustained a heavy loss, and we desire hereby to express our appreciation of his worth as a man, and a faithful and devoted teacher.*

Increasing Interest.

It would be impossible, except by swelling this volume to a size not contemplated by the Institute when authorizing its publication, to give in the preceding synopsis of meetings the numerous details which would be alike interesting and instructive. A summary of the essential portions of the many lectures and addresses delivered by eminent educators, would have been an invaluable contribution to educational literature, and the practical ideas contained in them would have been found important aids in the school-room. A reference, however, to the various topics discussed, cannot fail

---

*Mr. Gamwell was born in Peru, Massachusetts, October 29th, 1816. He was educated at Brown University, and graduated in September, 1817. He immediately afterwards accepted an appointment as Principal of the Fountain Street Grammar School in Providence, subsequently transferred to the new building on Federal Street, a position he occupied with distinguished success until his labors were terminated by fatal disease. He died December 18th, 1871, in the peaceful trust inspired by the christian faith his life had so consistently illustrated. He left a wife and four children to mourn an event which awakened the sorrow of a wide circle of friends. A fine portrait of Mr. Gamwell hangs in the Hall of the Federal Street Grammar school house.

to suggest to teachers trains of thought helpful in the discharge of their responsible and often perplexing duties. The questions upon which these lectures and addresses were based, will, for the most part, suggest the desired answers, and a careful perusal of this synopsis of Institute work, will, in this particular, be found highly advantageous.

'It is especially interesting to trace through the years covered by the brief history thus far presented, the influence of the annual and subsidiary meetings of the Institute in multiplying friends to the cause of popular education, and in strengthening its hold upon the public mind. This is made evident by the increased attendance upon its meetings, as well as by the high character of the citizens who extended to them their cordial support. This has been a more distinctly marked feature within the last fourteen years. Up to that time, with few exceptions, and those were evenings when a popular speaker from abroad addressed the Institute, the vestry of a church had furnished all needed accommodations. But year by year the circle of interest widened until in 1870 it became necessary to transfer the annual meetings to Roger Williams Hall, capable of seating sixteen hundred people. A single year demonstrated that even this Hall was of too limited dimensions, and in 1872, for this reason, the evening exercises were held in Music Hall, the largest audience room in Providence, if not in the State. The annual meetings of 1873 and 1874, held in this latter hall, were pre-eminently distinguished for numbers and enthusiasm. Such gatherings of teachers and the friends of education were never before seen in Rhode Island, if indeed, in any part of the United States. At the evening sessions, each year, not less than three thousand persons were present.

The *ninety-ninth* meeting of the Institute, being the TWENTY-NINTH ANNUAL MEETING, was held as above stated, January 9th, 10th and 11th, 1873.

Election of Officers.

The forenoon of Thursday (9th) was devoted by members to visiting the State Normal School and the Providence

High School. In the afternoon, from two to four o'clock, the Grammar, Intermediate, and Primary schools of the city were visited, to witness the usual exercises in each.

At 2 o'clock, P. M., a session of the Department of Higher Instruction was held in the Providence High School. The object of this session was stated by the President, (Mr. Lyon,) to be "to secure to the teachers of the higher schools the same advantages that the teachers of other schools had at the annual meetings of the Institute.* The following papers were then read: "Methods of Teaching the Classics," by Professor Albert Harkness, of Brown University; "The Importance of Mathematical Studies to Literary Pursuits," by Professor Benjamin F. Clarke, of Brown University. The reading of these papers was followed by animated and instructive discussions, which were participated in by Charles B. Goff, Edward H. Cutler, O. H. Kile, N. W. Littlefield, David W. Hoyt, William A. Mowry, Thomas B. Stockwell, and Edwin M. Stone. In the evening a large audience assembled at Music Hall, when an able address on "The Criterion of Education," was delivered by Hon. E. E. White, of Columbus, Ohio.

Friday morning, an address of welcome was delivered by Rev. Henry W. Rugg, of the Providence School Committee, and responded to in appropriate words by President Lyon. Professor Samuel S. Greene, of Brown University, read a paper on "Thought and Expression:"

Thought was placed first, because it was really first in time and importance: expression second in time and the necessary instrument by which thought is made known. Thought is to be gained by direct effort, expression by indirect, which united gives us language. Every person in common life needs to know how to speak and write his own language with correctness and some degree of elegance. How can our children be taught to do this in our common schools? Not by the study of text-

*The school visitations commenced in 1871, and meetings of the "Department of Higher Instruction," begun in 1873, were new features in the arrangements for the annual meetings of the Institute. In 1874 a Grammar and Primary school section was added.

10

books in the science of Grammar alone or chiefly. but by such training as shall stimulate thought and lead to its expression, care being taken to give thought its legitimate place. that of supremacy over expression. A child should not be led to think by unwise criticisms of the style of his penmanship. grammar, spelling, etc , that the expression is first in importance. Tell a child to go and examine or witness something within his comprehension, and then let him tell it his own way, and give him the impression that his thought is of the most importance. Children should be taught to think and read for a definite object, and when this is accomplished the expression will be acquired. Do not demand of a child an original composition. without preparing his mind by leading him into the right thought. All school exercises should be made a means of teaching correct expression of earnest thought.

This paper elicited an instructive discussion. participated in by Professor Joseph Eastman, Rev. Daniel Leach. Superintendent of Providence Public Schools. Professor Greene, Hon. E. E. White. Commissioner Thomas W. Bicknell. and Rev. Edwin M. Stone. A pleasant exercise in "Gymnastics." was given by a class of pupils from the Thayer Street Grammar School. under the direction of Miss Margaret L. Phillips. The accuracy and gracefulness of the drill. excited the admiration of the audience.

The afternoon exercises were opened with singing by five hundred pupils belonging to the several Grammar Schools of the city. under the direction of Mr. B. W. Hood. The pieces. five in number. were finely rendered. showing careful training on the part of the teacher. Pupils from the State Normal School gave exercises in Reading. conducted by Professor L. B. Monroe. These exercises were well sustained throughout. and gave great satisfaction. Professor J. Lewis Diman delivered a scholarly and instructive address on "The Teacher's Culture." Hon. E. E. White spoke in approval of the sentiments advanced. and Rev. Mr. Ela, of East Greenwich, presented briefly. "The Means by which Real Culture may be Obtained." Professor Monroe read the "Pied Piper of Hamlin."

In the evening the hall was crowded to overflowing. Addresses were made by Governor Seth Padelford, Hon. Thos.

A. Doyle, Mayor of Providence, Hon. John Kingsbury, Rev. Dr. Robinson, President of Brown University, Hon. E. E. White, Hon. Henry Barnard, and Hon. Thomas W. Bicknell. Professor Monroe read three poems, which were received with great applause. The excellent music for the evening was furnished by about one hundred and fifty female High School pupils, under the direction of Mr. B. W. Hood, Mr. Frank F. Tingley presiding at the organ.

Saturday forenoon the meeting was mainly devoted to business. Besides the election of officers and the customary votes of thanks, resolutions were passed recommending a modification of the district system of this State, approving State representation by one or more Commissioners at the International Industrial Exposition to be held in Vienna, Austria, in the summer and autumn of 1873, and recognizing elementary Natural History "as a necessary fundamental department of public instruction." The following resolutions are among the number presented and adopted :

Resolved, That no system of education can be considered complete which does not provide for girls the same educational advantages boys now enjoy, and that, in the opinion of the members of this Institute, the cause of education will be advanced in this State when its daughters can obtain within its borders the highest education.

Resolved, That we have learned with profound regret of the decease of Professor C. M. Alvord, of East Greenwich Seminary, whose long and faithful service, and distinguished success in the work of a teacher, have commanded the admiration of his fellow-teachers, as his pure and noble christian character has secured the respect and love of all who have been permitted to know his worth.*

The Committee on the Institute Manual reported that the work would be in readiness for the press in the course of a few weeks.

The committee to whom was referred the subject of the *Rhode Island Schoolmaster*, reported, and recommended

* Professor Caleb M. Alvord, was born in East Hampton, Mass., May 3d, 1815, and died at East Greenwich, R. I., January 6th, 1873, aged fifty-eight years.

" that the journal be continued as heretofore under the editorial direction of the School Commissioner, and the business management of Mr. T. B. Stockwell," with a Board of twelve contributing editors. The recommendation was adopted.

Adjourned.

The several sessions of the Institute, from the commencement to the close, were of an elevated character, and of unusual interest. The addresses, lectures and papers, opened fresh and valuable truths to the minds of all present, and to the inspiration of great ideas was added the inspiration of the crowd that daily thronged the hall.

The *one hundredth meeting* of the Institute, being also the THIRTIETH ANNUAL MEETING, opened in Providence, January 22d, 1874, and continued until noon of the 24th. The forenoon of the first day (Thursday) was, as in the three preceding years, devoted to visiting the schools of the city, together with the State Normal School. In the afternoon two meetings of teachers and others were held in the High School Building, viz.: "The Department of Higher Instruction," and "The Grammar and Primary School Section." The former was presided over by Professor Joseph Eastman, of the Conference Seminary at East Greenwich, and the latter by Mr. L. W. Russell, Principal of the Bridgham School in Providence. Both meetings were largely attended by the most prominent educators of the city and the State. The latter was crowded to excess. The Department of Higher Instruction commenced its session with a paper by Mr. David W. Hoyt, Principal of the English and Scientific Department for boys in the Providence High School, on "The Relation of the Teacher to Modern Progress in Physical Science." The following is an abstract:

The teacher is the interpreter who stands between the original investigator and the people. All acknowledge the power of the press as an educator. Popular lectures by masters in science afford entertainment and awaken interest; but the next generation of men and women will owe most of its permanent ideas in science to the teachers and the textbooks of to-day.

It is the duty of the teacher to keep himself informed of the recent progress made in science. One who has ceased to learn should cease to teach. The progress of science furnishes the mental food needed to fit one for his duties, even though he may not directly teach that which he learns; but his knowledge of recent discoveries should be more minute and extensive, in proportion as they bear more directly upon the branches he is called to teach.

There is a broad distinction between what the teacher ought to *know*, and what he ought to *teach*. Two evils, of an opposite character, beset his calling:—

1. Teaching the old, simply because it is old, and the teacher thoroughly understands it; and neglecting to teach the new, simply because it is new, and the teacher is too old or too lazy to learn it himself. We often misjudge of the relative value or difficulty of the old and the new methods. The old is so thoroughly a part of ourselves that we fail to realize that both are equally unknown to our pupils.

2. Teaching the new, simply because it is new, and neglecting to teach what is comparatively old, simply because it is old. While the fossil teacher may be guilty of the error first mentioned, the progressive teacher is liable to commit this one. The temptation is two-fold. First, it is easy to teach with interest and enthusiasm what one has just learned. The success of young teachers is often due to this fact. We are all young in our recent acquirements, and it is well that it is so; we only plead that we should use our judgment as well as our personal enthusiasm in determining what to teach. The second temptation is furnished by public examinations. Committees and the public may be interested in what is novel, though old but important subjects are neglected.

The present importance of a subject is one point to be considered in determining whether it should be taught. The multitude of wrecked theories, and even practical chemical processes, which lie along the stream of time, are now of little importance, except as items of history.

The amount of time at the disposal of the teacher is, in most cases, unfortunately, the most important practical point to be considered. Let us, however, suppose, for the moment, that the selection of topics is to be made upon other grounds. We pass, then, to consider our principal proposition.

New discoveries and theories should not be introduced into a course of academic instruction till they are firmly established. Even the pioneers of thought and discovery must admit this. The text-book and the teacher are not only the interpreters, but the great conservative power.

It may be asked, why should the teacher study these, if he is not expected to teach them? The reasons which pertain to his own mental growth and character have already been given. The pupil has enough to occupy his mind in what is firmly established. The teacher should be able to exercise the judicial spirit, neither believing nor disbelieving till he has sufficient reason therefor. The average pupil is incapable of such a state of mind; he blindly believes. These new discoveries and theo-

ries may soon become so fully established that the teacher will be expected to include them in his course of instruction; and even if he does
not teach them directly, they may modify his teaching. Again, there are
students whom the "average pupil" does not represent. A few will seek
from the teacher information in regard to the questions of the day.

The remainder of the paper consisted of a practical application of the principle above enunciated, naming some subjects which, in the judgment of the author, may be taught,
and others which are not yet so well understood as to be properly included in a course of academical training. It continues :

The revelations made by spectrum analysis are wonderful, enabling,
as it does, the celestial chemist to analyze the heavenly bodies. But how
much of the application of spectrum analysis to the heavenly bodies
should we be justified in teaching at present? Perhaps little more than
this: The bright lines of a spectrum indicate the character of the gases
from which the light comes, and the dark lines the nature of the gases
through which it comes.

The spectroscope has revealed enough to overturn some of the old
theories respecting the physical constitution of the sun; but we know
little more about it than this: The sun is surrounded by an immense
gaseous atmosphere, containing sundry elements, some of which are
found, also, on the earth.

The greatest changes of the last few years have been in the *theories*
adopted. New facts have been added to the common stock, but the old
ones cannot be thrown aside, like old theories. One department is of too
much importance to be passed over in silence. It includes what is spoken
of as "conversion of energy," "conservation of force," or the "correla-
tion of forces,"—not only the theories of what were once called the im-
ponderable agents, such as heat, light, and electricity, but also, in a
wider sense, those of gravity, cohesion, and chemical affinity,—in fact,
the unity of force and of natural phenomena, and perchance, of matter
itself. Not many years since the tendency of the times was to multiply
chemical elements and forces in physical science, as well as species in
natural history. Now men are not only striving to prove a common
origin for species, but some are seeking to trace all physical forces to a
common source, and all kinds of matter to the same original substance.

Teachers should accept it as a fact that a thermal unit is equivalent to
seven hundred and seventy-two foot-pounds; that is, the force which
would raise a given weight of water one degree Fahrenheit, would lift
the same weight seven hundred and seventy-two feet. We teach that
light and heat consist in vibrations of atoms or molecules; that light is
transmitted to us from the sun by the vibrations of the ether. Probably
electricity should also be regarded as a mode of atomic or molecular mo-

tion; but just how the motion differs from that of light and heat we cannot say. Electricity is evidently convertible into heat, light, and mechanical force; but the duty of teachers is plainly to await future developments on this subject. So far as gravity, cohesion, and chemical affinity are concerned, we have no theory to teach. Why matter thus attracts other matter we cannot tell, even though Saigey and others attempt to account for these forces by the vibration and rotation of molecules of matter carrying with them atmospheres of ethereal atoms.

The unity of force leads naturally to the unity of matter. Some evolutionists would make the ether the original of all matter; others would make the original atoms of two kinds, ethereal and corporeal, with, perhaps, hydrogen as the original of the corporeal; others still, would recognize some or all the chemical elements as originally distinct forms of corporeal matter. As teachers, we propose still to treat the chemical elements as distinct, even though we are forced to resort to allotropism and isomerism.

The subject presented in this paper was learnedly discussed by Mr. Isaac F. Cady, of Barrington, and Professors S. S. Greene and B. F. Clarke, of Brown University. After a brief recess, Professor J. L. Lincoln, of Brown University, read a thoughtful and discriminating paper on "Preparatory Classical Studies," in which he considered their value and the spirit and method of pursuing them. He would not place classical studies in antagonism to the physical sciences. Physical science generally addresses the understanding. It is the office of literature to reach the soul, and thus the Iliad of Homer supplies a felt want.

The study of language cultivates fixed and concentrated attention. The ancient languages are more perfect and regular than the modern, but have a family relation to all the modern tongues, and are not *dead*. Latin still lives in the French, Spanish, English and Italian languages. Greek and Latin still speak with ever-living voices. The study of these languages is a means to an end. We are to seek culture from their literatures. In their thoughts and subjects they inspire us to spiritual worth. They teach precepts of truth. They are still unapproached in literary excellence. Hence you have a sufficient argument for the value of classical studies in a liberal education.

The pupil should have a clear and sure aim of what he is to do and be. The languages should be learned and acquired; made a lasting possession of the mind. We all need to try more and more to achieve the positive results of better learning by the use of the existing good methods of study. These languages should be mastered for our use. This can be done " *Possunt quia posse vicentur,*" I mean by *mastering* just what we mean by mastering a modern language which we purpose to use in reading and speaking. We should put Professor Harkness' excellent works to practical use in constantly interchanging Latin and English in all their forms, and by question and answer. No form or word but should be coined into living speech. The book should only be given up when the scholar has it all in his mind. With what facility might you then read a Latin author. Not only should book-words be used, but there should be something like conversation between teacher and scholar. The names of common objects and acts should be used in daily intercourse. You would not lose but gain time by it, making the school a *ludus* as in olden time. All this might be done without any letting down of grammatical strictness, but the pupil would come back with greater appetite for knowledge. The lesson should be read back from the translation into the original, and every new word made so familiar that it need not be learned again. Thus there would be a real progress in knowledge, and the end of classical study be obtained.

There are higher aims in the study of language; first, the teacher will strive to bring into his work a taste for literary beauty. It is a pleasure to so instruct the scholar, and to urge him to this study which has done so much for others. We should not regard language as mere material for grammatical analysis. We may begin the study too early, before we are able to appreciate their beauties and diction. Our pupils should know and feel these beauties, which they should study, not as tasks to be learned, but as noblest diversions for future days. They should be conversant with the authors and know their excellences. The work of translation should be made a means of discipline to the student in his own vernacular.

Again, the life of the people among whom Greek and Roman letters grew up should be a subject of study. Greek and Latin each contributed to the Christian religion, and here is a fruitful theme which should be of interest to the student in the early part of his study. What were their manners and customs, their relation to the races of modern times are subjects of a life-work which should be early begun. Virgil should be studied as a national poet, Cicero as an exponent of Roman political life. I am glad we have schools which do so good work, which have given so many good scholars to our University. I trust they will do yet better service. In reading not long since of the schools of England, I received some idea of the power of these schools in enlightening the nation, and I would say to our teachers, it is a worthy ambition to sustain the reputation of our schools. See to it that you adorn the Sparta of your dwelling-place. Devote the power it shall give you to virtue, truth and religion.

This paper was discussed by Mr. F. W. Tilton, Principal

of the High School in Newport, and Mr. Alonzo Williams, of the Friends School, Providence.

The Grammar and Primary Section was first addressed by the chairman, on some methods and mistakes in Reading.

Mr. J. C. Greenough, Principal of the State Normal School, then read a paper on the management of reading with young pupils.

He placed considerable stress upon the union of the powers or sounds of the letters forming the earliest words learned by the child; also, that the word should not be presented till the thing it symbolizes was known to the child, or the idea to be conveyed comprehended. He thought much was lost to the child by a want of freshness in the matter presented for reading lessons. He hoped to see the day when, to obviate this, printed sheets would be furnished monthly, by some competent committee chosen for the purpose, to be distributed among the schools of a State or community, these sheets to contain appropriate matter for different grades of schools, exciting curiosity in the children, by the continued newness, and affording the opportunity of keeping the children interested in current topics, in history, politics, discoveries, &c., which they could comprehend.

He thought the reading book a very important one. Around it clustered much in after years of school-life. The influence of the pieces and of the teacher's work when teaching them was very great.

He closed the paper by some eloquent allusions to the doors which may be opened to the pupils through the reading lessons to the gems of our great authors, forming and molding the tastes of the pupils for their works.

Two papers followed; one by Miss Mary A. Riley, of Westerly, on teaching "Elementary Geography," and the other by Miss Susan C. Bancroft, assistant teacher in the Normal School, on "Early Steps in Language."

Miss Riley regarded the teaching of position as of first importance. It should be done before the name Geography is uttered in the class, and by locating different objects in the school room, and speaking of their positions, absolute and as related to each other. Then the streets of the town, and houses, etc., located upon them might be taken up till the necessity of a map was felt. Then map drawing might be begun, rude at first, but to be perfected in the higher grades.

Miss Bancroft advocated the teaching of language in all the school lessons from the earliest period of school going, long before what is termed

20

composition-writing begins. The pupils should be taught to tell about the things they see and handle. Here is where they get their first lessons in language. She impressed upon the audience the great importance of the teacher's using correct language in all the lessons and conversations and aiding the pupils to do the same. People often come to serious misunderstanding and legal contests even by a misconception of words. The legal profession would be deprived of half their work were it not for this. Some useful hints of interest to teachers were given in relation to further steps in teaching language.

These papers were respectively discussed by Messrs Albert J. Manchester, J. Milton Hall, James M. Sawin, Rev. Daniel Leach, and Professor S. S. Greene, each presenting practical ideas, enhancing thereby to teachers the usefulness of the session.

The evening session at Music Hall attracted a large audience. President Lyon introduced Hon. John Eaton, United States Commissioner of Education, who delivered a lecture upon the general character of education, and some of its pressing needs.

In his introductory remarks the speaker quoted the words of Sir Walter Raleigh when lifting the axe of the executioner in the Tower of London, a short time before his execution. He said, "This is a sharp instrument, but it cures all diseases." His career and death, said he, were an illustration, and his words an expression of the sentiment of his days. But another treatment is now universally approved; indeed, the change was then at hand. Two years after his execution the settlement of New England marked a new departure. In spite of the times the course of events led to the formation of a government in which all, equal before their Divine Master, were equal before the law of the land. Our forefathers saw that their compact of government must allow the children to learn so much of letters as to be able to read the Bible and the laws under which they were to be governed. In the past, nations treated vice and crime by the sharp edge of the executioner's axe, but our fathers began to employ here in the wilderness a new remedy. They introduced education by the government compact, resulting in a civilization and in a nation that has presented before the world a spectacle of dealing successfully with actual treason without the execution of the traitor. Education neither begins nor ends with the book knowledge, but is only concentrated and intensified by the aid of teachers and books.

The lecturer spoke of education as affected by the necessary changes produced by the changes of time. Outside of New England, shortly after its settlement, instruction was, as a rule, under the control of the church or private individuals, and extended only to the few. At the day of this settlement, we look in vain for civil decrees or laws enforcing education. A century later, civil law in Russia decreed elementary education, but it was only because the people would by it be more efficient subjects of the monarchy. Outside of the inhospitable wilderness of the New World, education was given only to the few; but our fathers proposed to give all a chance to be educated, for they saw that vice and crime and poverty would be less frequent by its influence. They saw that all persons were endangered by these evils, and proposed they should all have the same chance to escape them. Our fathers saw that property could prevent vice, crime and pauperism by bearing the expense of education. Opposition to the continuation of the support of education forgets that each individual, each generation, must begin just as its predecessor. Man's work must not only be done anew and wholly, for each child as it appears, but each one must be informed and stimulated to do his part of the work of the town, the State, and the nation. The neglect of elementary training for five years in any community, would find the next generation on the stage totally ignorant. The thoughtful worker in the cause of education must have these considerations in view when he is counting the cost of sustaining systems of education in vigorous operation. Our predecessors formed their conclusions that property must be put into the cause of education, and if we do not wish to experience the civil upheavals common among uneducated nations in their day, we must hold in mind their conclusions.

The lecturer then went on to consider the effects of changes in the population on educational questions.

A thing absolutely essential to the success of the work of the school is the intelligent and sympathetic coöperation of the surrounding community. When this is wanting and the teacher feels compelled not only to stimulate the pupils in their own efforts, and iterate and reiterate to them the things which should be brought before them by their parents and friends, there is but little hope of success.

In conclusion the speaker addressing himself to the school teachers of Rhode Island, said, if I have not directed my remarks successfully to you this evening, if I have rather suggested facts, the consideration of which should be for the whole American people, and should inspire every parent and citizen with an anxious and sympathetic coöperation; still I have not forgotten that the success or failure is committed to you. Have you taken your position from right motives? Are you in the line of duty? The Great Master says to you "go on," and His protection and support will not fail you.

At the close of the lecture, Professor Mark Bailey, of Yale College, read the re-union poem, by Holmes, a selection from Dombey and Son, including the death of little Paul, and the story of the Hoosier who invested in live oysters, all of which were received with strong marks of satisfaction; and thus closed the first day of unusual intellectual enjoyment.

Friday morning (second day) the Institute was opened with devotional exercises by Rev. D. H. Greer, Rector of Grace Church. President Lyon made an earnest and appropriate address of welcome to the teachers assembled from every part of the State, and representing the interests of education in their respective towns.

The high mission to which the teachers of to-day are called, is a cause for congratulation. Their duties are worthy of the most exalted talents, the most cultivated intellects, and the noblest aspirations. Their work is not merely a profession, but a calling to which they are summoned by a *vox interna*, whose bidding they cannot disregard. Under its influence they should consecrate all the powers of their being,—physical, mental, and spiritual. To elevate and ennoble their chosen pursuit should be the inspiring motive to untiring efforts, until, from exhausted energies, they are unable to perform its responsible and self-denying labors. In Germany, where the profession has received its highest honor and won its noblest victories, teachers who have taught forty years in the public schools, retire on full pay.

President Lyon then adverted to the different topics to be discussed and to the general arrangements for the meetings of the Institute, as well calculated to bring out the best thoughts of those who should speak, and to make this meeting of the Institute a profitable one to all in attendance.

At the close of his address, Mr. J. C. Greenough was introduced to the audience, and read a paper upon "The Use of Text-Books."

He defined a text-book as a book regularly used by the student in the preparation of his lesson. Text-books are of different qualities, but we are to consider when a good text-book should or should not be used. They should not be used when the printed page will not convey what is to be taught. Early teaching must be without books, and first ideas are the most important since they determine the pupil's future acquirements. Words are not the objects of our knowledge, but principles, and principles are facts systematically arranged. We must study facts before we can classify. The perceptive faculties develop first in order, and upon their development depends that of the other faculties. Something more than words are needed to develop this faculty. We must have objects to teach, and teach the objects before the words. The teacher should distinguish between telling and teaching. He should observe and then make his own statements. This was Agassiz's method. The pupil gaining ideas in the natural order will adopt this method in after life, and will investigate for himself. This will make individual men rather than machines. Some say it is well to fix correct statements and store the mind with facts, to be known in later years; but this cultivates a habit of trusting to statements and memory rather than to experience. Let the teacher direct the pupil's investigation of his own consciousness. This is more properly called the natural method.

When text-books contain the things to be studied—as language, literature, and the like, they must be used. We should save time by increase of interest, acting as original investigators. There is a prejudice in many minds against oral teaching which is just, if it refers to mere rambling talk. Teaching should be brief, concise and thoroughly understood by the teacher. Such teaching awakens enthusiasm. Books containing problems are useful, but principles and rules should be taught orally. Books often present the subject in such a manner that the need of observation is not felt. Teaching is the mark of teachers not of text books.

Text-books may be used to gain knowledge which cannot be obtained by experience, as in history and geography. Single facts are of little value except in their relation to other facts and to principles. The teacher should lead the pupil to compare known facts and reach conclusions valuable to himself and others. The pupil should study things before principles and statements, should be familiar with practice before learning rules. In the study of language, translation precedes the methods of grammar. When the pupil has come to understand the subject, if text-books can best state the knowledge, they may be profitably used.

The views presented in this paper were discussed at considerable length by Rev. Carlton A. Staples, Rev. Daniel Leach, and Professor Samuel S. Greene. Mr. Staples complimented the paper, and referred to his former teacher, who was wont to say "no one was fit to teach unless he could dispense with the text-books." He continued:

There is a difference in pupils about using text-books. If we consider the aim to impart knowledge of facts and fit the scholar for life's work by awakening habits of thoughtfulness we shall arrive at proper conclusions. While the intellect should be cultivated, it is also important that facts and principles, which prepare the pupil to fill his place in life, should likewise be imparted, and this must be done mainly by text-books, even if the teacher make his own books.

The majority of pupils have not and never can have much individuality and to teach such pupils we must rely on text-books. Spelling must be learned by memory, it cannot be reasoned out, and in grammar we must teach principles from text-books. The reasoning powers should be developed; but, after all, do we not rely chiefly on the memory, even though it be treacherous? We do not succeed in properly awakening moral and religious life even in our Sunday schools; we should not only learn the rules but form the habits of virtuous conduct. So, in the intellectual life, we may simply cram the memory with facts. This is better than nothing, but not what is needed. We are gaining in illustration and in striving to awaken thoughtfulness and interest. It is more difficult to teach without text-books and to make a good exhibition to the trustees, commissioners and parents, yet a very little power of discrimination is better than any amount of mere book knowledge.

Rev. Mr. Leach followed Mr. Staples, and said:

He believed a skillful teacher would not be closely confined to text-books, but properly used they are essential to the good of the school. How they should be used would depend upon the capacity, age and circumstances of the child. Thought may be awakened by objects, by pictures, by description, or by the names of objects. Children have few spontaneous ideas, and early knowledge is limited; how, then, can a teacher present numerous objects? The more the teacher can use objects the better, but pictures, descriptions or names of objects must at times take their place. Without the names of objects he will know nothing of what he sees. Thoughts must be put into language and should be extracted from language. The child that can do this readily and accurately is educated. The memory is the only conservator of knowledge, and this is by exact, definite, precise language. Thoughts should be, as far as possible, in logical order; the closer the intimacy of relation the better The cultivation of memory should not be the exclusive work in our schools. A difficult but profitable work is the expression of thoughts in different words from those through which they were received. Reasoning is the comparison of facts and is entirely dependent on the memory. To criticise is easy; a man might state just how to make a watch, and yet not be able to construct one. We all desire to give the pupil as much knowledge as possible, and teach him to use it in the most effective manner. Words and language must be furnished before many ideas can be communicated, but the mind should not be burdened with mere empty words. Pupils should use pencil and slate, giving, in their own words, the ideas received.

I dissent from the view that definitions and principles should be left to the teacher. It would produce confusion, and we should have no fixed definitions. The most difficult part of teaching, and that which requires the most skill, is to express principles accurately and concisely in language, and when done these should be preserved. One defect in our teaching is inexactness. Processes should precede definitions but knowledge should be preserved in the best language. As regards spelling words the pupil does not understand, it is impossible that he should understand the full meaning of all the words he meets. Children should thus learn to use words accurately. The memorizing of words is to be learned primarily by young pupils from sentences in their reading lesson and by using them to express thoughts of their own. In reading we have the mechanical process and also the intellectual. The latter extracts the thought from the page. We next put thought into language and make it effective to others. We wish to cultivate the memory that the pupil may reason. Oral teaching is apt to be given at random. As a rule we should teach only what applies to the lesson. Beginning at the foundation all knowledge should be related. We should not burden the memory with useless knowledge. When the memory is gone, all is gone. It is well to make knowledge attractive, but let the pupil understand that it is by toil and effort only that knowledge i gained. The mind as well as well as the body needs strong meat. We never read of a man who attained eminence as a scholar who had not a good memory. Our teachers are now striving more than ever, that the scholars shall derive ideas from the text-books and not that they may give a mere verbal recitation.

Professor Greene, in closing the discussion, said :

I belong to both sides of this question. In my earlier years of study the professor came before us with notes or books and began to rub a glass tube with a calf-skin. He then held it over the table on which he had placed some light particles and we saw these alternately attracted to and repelled from the glass. He then began to explain it and give us facts connected with it. I enjoyed this exercise, I know I did. I can conceive of his coming with the statement of the fact and then proving his statement by experiments. I sometimes question which is the better, but I confess I like the first. I should not wish the professor to repeat it many times. Object-teaching is often carried to excess.

Suppose I take geography; I wish to give the pupil an idea of Madagascar I first show him an island, however small, then teach him of larger islands, and go from the object which gives the elementary idea up to the great idea. If you say to me, " Titus erected a battering ram," unless I have seen a picture of it, it is all a grand *blank* to me. The object of teaching is to fill out and open up the thoughts which the pupil entrusts to memory. Commit to memory through the understanding, not through the language simply. My thought is this; the business of the teacher is to furnish ideas, let him use text-books, but let him make his ideas clear. The disadvantage of teaching without a tex-book is the crowding into the mind of five or six different things without a record. A record helps to recall. It should be as brief as possible. My class are required to take their own notes or to take my dictation, I have tried this method and am satisfied. The text-book must have a great deal of *lum-*

ber in it; let me use the book and throw away the lumber. Both with
and without the text-book, is the true way to teach; the teacher who
cannot teach without, is not fit to teach.

Professor Bailey gave a pleasant lecture on Reading:

I occasionally find a class well drilled in logical analysis, and this is
the preparation for reading sentences. Do you not think it possible to
make reading orderly, scientific and more useful and practical? Huxley
says, " Method is the same in all sciences." Observe facts, then group,
and then elaborate them. Deducing conclusions from this elaborating of
facts, you individualize and observe the points of similarity. You then
test your observations. This is verification. This method is not impossible in reading. We may go out and observe the best talkers, we observe the same facts in the conversations of many, and then say, " All
persons speak in this way " For example, how do people speak when
most happy in expression? On matter of fact ideas, they speak just loud
enough, and just fast enough, with moderate force, stress, time, &c. We
thus begin to classify. What changes are made for increased enthusiasm?
Their ideas are expressed faster, louder and with marked stress. You
know expressions of joy or sorrow, when you cannot hear the words.
We observe, till we are satisfied, how people express happy ideas. Joy-
ous ideas are spoken with gushing emphasis, increased time, a longer
slide, and purer quality of voice. We observe sadness in the same way.
We have here also good training in accurate observation. People when
sad, use the semi-tone, as we use the black keys of an instrument for
plaintive pieces. It is a law of nature in speech as well as in music, that
we should use suppressed force and peculiar half tones to indicate sadness. Grand, royal words, require large volume and open tone. Pleasant
language for harsh ideas is not always sufficient. They require far different tones. abrupt emphasis, harsh stress. The dog will mind when you
speak decidedly. He will generally mind the tone of voice rather than
the words spoken. You distinguish irony by the tone, if you hear it, or
by the sentiment, if you read. It is a difficult thing to individualize
ideas, but this is the secret of good reading. Note the points of resem-
blance or difference. The first means of individualization is by comparison and contrast; all thought depends on these. Everything is relative.
You must have lights and shadows in expression and in thinking. Our
bad reading is not due to the want of good voices, but to a want of careful thought and accurate preparation.

At the afternoon session Professor Bailey resumed his lecture, and read with the pupils of the Normal School, President Lincoln's speech delivered at Cemetery Hill, bringing
out the contrasts, and showing that a phrase containing but a

single idea should be spoken as a whole, and tested his directions for emphasis and stress. The exercise was one of the best features of this department of instruction, and was received by the audience with unqualified satisfaction.

At the close of Professor Bailey's lecture, Mr. Levi W. Russell read a paper upon the question, "How can our Schools be Improved?" He said :

This question can hardly be considered distinct from the whole work we have discussed here. But as I understand the point, it is to bring to light the faults of our schools with a view to rectifying them. And we shall not lack advisers, for every Yankee can run the government or teach a school. The reformer says: " All is out of joint." Everything is to be done by method and made perfect.

Then there are the specialists of divers kinds. The professions come to us: the physician, attorney, painter, sculptor, trader, the master mechanic, and even the kitchen, invades the school. The pressure for more and better is so great we may well pause and ask if our schools are adapted to the pupil. So many things require study just when the pupil needs time and opportunity for physical development. Music, drawing, sketching, &c., the natural sciences, to say nothing of history and declamation, are urged upon us. New studies improve the appearance of the school, but the question arises, will they not kill the scholars, especially the girls? It is not difficult to urge them to work beyond recuperation. The boy generally manages to live through it, and takes to mental growth afterward. The tendency is to keep all we have and add more. It will take but a few minutes each day, and is so important. Is not our present system injurious? What can best be spared, is the question. Make music recreation, let drawing in part replace writing. With the haste of fathers and mothers it is plain we cannot lengthen the time. We should concentrate attention on a few studies and be thorough. Facts are worth more than theories. My own experience in Spelling teaches that it can be learned thoroughly. In Geography, we should teach how to use maps rather than make use of them ourselves. In Arithmetic we give too much work. Our school work requires too long application to be healthfully accomplished, but who is to blame for this? Ask the mothers and fathers who will urge their children forward. Ask the school visitors. We are all to blame and must mend, or our pupils will be physical wrecks. The time is at hand. In Hartford and Boston the movement of reform has begun. Children under fifteen years old should do most of their studying in school during school hours. You may say these hours are not all devoted to study; part of the time is taken in recitations; but recitations should require as much mental application as study. There are manifest and important advances, as in grading and classification, but there are objections to a close adherence to these. The com-

11

mittee and teacher expect the same from every scholar. Nothing is more impossible, unless the requirements are low. Many a teacher will keep back some for the others. Would it not be better that even the dull scholars should make progress? I do not advocate a superficial course, but that the pupil learn thoroughly what his mental ability is fitted for.

Mr. Russell advocated the presence of women on School Boards, and more male teachers in schools of lower grades, that the pupils might come into contact with the masculine mind. The two should work together in mental training. To improve our schools only teachers entirely qualified for their duties should be employed. Skilled teachers should be promoted and well paid, outranking those who do a minimum of work for maximum pay. The Germans say to us, " You build palaces for school houses, and starve your teachers." It is not nearly so bad as they represent, but when you pay better wages, you will get better teachers and have better schools.

Mr. Russell's paper was discussed by Mr. William A. Mowry :

We may all have our theories, but for myself, I *know* less about it than I thought I did ten years ago. Let us see what elements constitute a good school. First, a good teacher; second, good scholars; third, interested parents; fourth, the school house and its appliances; fifth, the methods of study.

As regards good scholars, we should not give the most attention to teaching the best, but the poorest. We cannot choose our material. Proper attention should be given to ventilation, heating, light, text-books, &c. The good sense of the people will look after these matters. Of the course of study I know little. The basis seems to be the same as our fathers studied : the three " R's," with spelling, geography and grammar. Of methods, teachers have had pet theories which they have tried to prove a success, but which have not succeeded. Is it reasonable that we should spend as much time as our fathers upon these common studies, and have nothing of natural history and the botany of New England? I would not pull down the old till a better method can replace it. Would that the combined wisdom of New England might lay out a course of study for our schools. There is no profession where more mistakes are made. We spoil souls in learning how to teach, and don't learn then. The more I think of it, the more dissatisfied I am, but I do not see how to lay down a perfect course of study. A scheme will not be devised by mere local trials. Teachers should not take what is said from the plat-

form as perfect. It appears to me that a great mistake is made by at-
tempting to exhaust a subject the first time going over it. Would it not
be a better plan to go over the elements of a subject, as arithmetic, or
geography, or grammar, and then review, adding more difficult examples, and by the third time over, take all the intricate parts, thus com-
pleting the subject. Over half the pupils in our lower grades of schools
leave before arriving at the Grammar school. It appears to me that it
is better to take the elements of the " four ground rules," and proceed
with simple and easy examples through the elements of fractions and
decimals, United States money, and reduction and compound numbers,
perhaps even to percentage, before entering the Grammar school. Then
go back and review, adding more difficult problems and examples.
Every elementary study should be learned in this way—first, a cursory
view, then a more thorough *review*. Get first the leading points, then go
over again and get the details. We should ever keep in mind the primary
object of a course of school education. It is not the acquisition of
knowledge, that is secondary, but it is to develop and discipline the
powers of the mind ; to make strong men and women, with good heads
and good hearts.

The interest awakened by the exercises of the preceding
days had now reached a point of rare intensity. As the
hour for the evening session drew near, crowds were seen
hurrying to the Hall, as if fearful of failing to obtain a seat ;
and not without reason. At half past seven o'clock every
seat on the floor and in the spacious galleries was occupied.
Then the aisles began to fill, until they were densely packed,
while the vestibule and the entrance ways even to the street
were filled with persons striving in vain to gain admission.
This standing multitude stood patiently and quietly for more
than two hours listening with eager ears to the distinguished
gentlemen by whom the assembly was addressed—the silence
being broken only by repeated bursts of applause. It was a
proud moment for the members of the Institute, particularly
for those present who were among its founders, and who had
watched with parental solicitude its progress for nearly a
generation of years ; and as the President and the gentlemen
seated with him upon the platform looked down upon the
" sea of upturned faces," they evidently felt the quickening
power of the scene. The President addressed the assembly
in a few earnest words :

The presence of so great numbers was an assurance of their earnest sympathy in the cause of popular education. By it, teachers are cheered and stimulated to greater exertion. The proper training and culture of the young are worthy of the deepest interest and fostering care of all. The waywardness of youth, the alluring attractions of social life, and the seductive influence of worthless books, are obstacles which cannot be overcome by the teacher alone;—the task is too difficult, the labor too great. The cordial support and coöperation of parents and guardians are indispensable. Even the improved condition of our schools is but the golden fruitage of an elevated public opinion. This opinion has expressed itself in the increasingly liberal appropriations for education made. that without money and without price the best possible advantages may be given to every child in this State, thus opening wide the portals to the temple of knowledge. For the year ending June, 1836, the entire amount expended in this State for the support of public schools was only seven thousand four hundred and sixty-one dollars and ninety-nine cents. For 1873 it was six hundred and two thousand eight hundred and twelve dollars and twenty-eight cents—more than eighty times as much as it was thirty-seven years ago.

Yet the work is scarcely commenced. Rhode Island, if she would be true to her history, thoughtful of her highest welfare, and become, as Dr. Wayland once expressed it, the " Attica of America," must pour out her treasure like water. that her educational advantages make keep pace with her increasing wealth and general prosperity.

The other speakers of the evening were Lieutenant-Governor C. C. Van Zandt, Hon. Thomas A. Doyle, Rev. E. G. Robinson, D. D., President of Brown University, Hon. John Eaton, Rt. Rev. Thomas M. Clark, and Hon. Thomas W. Bicknell.

Lieutenant-Governor Van Zandt gave a vivid and amusing description of public schools as they existed in former years.

Mayor Doyle spoke of several changes he thought would eventually be made in the present school system. He was in favor of the assignment of fewer pupils to a teacher, and of giving to the woman who teaches the same studies as the man and does the work as well, the same compensation. He thought that there should be more school houses and smaller ones.

President Robinson compared the present method of teaching in our schools and colleges with that pursued four or five hundred years ago. He did not think well of crowding more studies into the school or the University than could be thoroughly mastered within a given time.   He expressed himself as in sympathy with a broad culture, and hoped that ere long there might be established a more vital union between Brown University and the common school system of the State.

Hon. John Eaton spoke of the increase of illiteracy, extending against an increase of wealth and prosperity in our own and in foreign lands.   He was gratified with the efforts making in Rhode Island to counteract this evil, and believed that gatherings like these of the Institute, and this sympathy of feeling in educational matters, would help the work throughout the country.

Bishop Clark, after referring to his early experience as a school teacher, called attention to the broad distinction between instruction and education.   Teachers often failed to notice this in their work.   He favored smaller schools and a larger number of teachers, and advocated the milder mode of school discipline.

Hon. Thomas W. Bicknell gave a comprehensive statement of what was doing for public instruction in Rhode Island. The number of weeks of schooling has been increased.   The compensation of teachers is better than formerly.   Permanency and stability were becoming elements in school work. The University and the Normal School were doing a great work for the State.   The wealth of Rhode Island, in proportion to population, is greater than that of any other New England State.   To make the schools better a better supervision throughout the State is needed.   Other wants are woman's influence on School Boards, a compulsory school law, an industrial school, a good truant law, a child-operative law, and a strong public sentiment to sustain it.

These addresses were interspersed with admirable music by the young ladies of the Providence High School, under the direction of Mr. B. W. Hood, Mr. Frank F. Tingley presiding at the organ.   Professor Bailey also read selections from Mark Twain's "Roughing It," from Mrs. H. B.

Stowe's "Oldtown Stories," and from Major Little's "Anthony and Cleopatra." The young ladies of the High School closed the exercises with the pleasant song, "Home, Sweet Home," and thus ended a day of great intellectual enjoyment.

At the closing meeting on Saturday forenoon, the Treasurer's report was received and accepted. Mr. Greenough, in a few appreciative words, announced the death of Prof. Osceola H. Kile, Principal of the High School in Westerly, and offered the following resolution, which was unanimously adopted by a silent vote, the members of the Institute rising:

Resolved, That in the death of Professor O. H. Kile, of Westerly, we have lost an able, enthusiastic and devoted teacher, who was equally remarkable for his success in the school-room and in the popular assembly.*

Mr. Samuel Austin read a short paper, replete with weighty thoughts, upon "The Importance and Demands of Elementary Education." After alluding to the great number of people who are not reached by popular education, he said:

Universal education is our boast, and might be our pride, if only we really provided it. It matters not whether it be pride or some other cause that closes our doors. Of those who do attend, two-thirds complete their education in the primary schools. The average attendance of our schools is very low. The uneducated form a large part of our population. A tide of foreign ignorance is constantly increasing the number. This fact should awaken deepest solicitude. The urgent demand is universal, thorough education. For this we should aim. President Robin-

* Mr. Kile was born in Lewis, Essex County, New York, January 16th, 1839, and died at Westerly, R. I., of pneumonia, January 16th, 1873. He was educated at the University of Vermont, and graduated in August, 1863. His earlier choice of a profession was the law, but subsequently determined to make teaching his life-business. His first effort was at Vergennes, Vt., where he built up a model school, and as an educator obtained an extensive influence in the State. He removed to Westerly in 1870, and became the Principal of the High School in that place. He attended the session of the Higher Department of Instruction at the opening of the annual meeting of the Institute, January 9th, 1873, but suffering from indisposition, was compelled to return home the same day, and survived only one week. He was highly esteemed for christian qualities by all who knew him, and his sudden death was widely mourned.

son well says that "candidates for the University are distinguished for
the thoroughness of their elementary education." The elementary education generally moulds the life. But even the ability to read has a great
influence upon after life. Our Reform School illustrates this fact. The
higher education will follow the elementary. Even from our evening
schools come aspirants for college training. The evening-schools are
doing a great work; they make good overseers instead of poor laborers.
Who can fathom our responsibility in view of the vast intellectual power
of the masses. The duty of providing for our native children is not the
most important. Does not the Christian system require the elevation of
the ignorant? Let us strive to comprehend something of the length,
height, depth and breadth of the subject. Shall we not compel the intellectually lame, halt and blind to come into our public schools? Our
material prosperity depends upon the prosperity of society. The rich
mines of education should be within reach of all classes. Let us multiply our attractive evening resorts, and thus cultivate the youth even
while they continue their daily toil.

Mr. Cady offered a resolution, approving of a proposition
to aid the common schools throughout the country by the dis-
tribution from the United States treasury of the net proceeds
of the public lands. The resolution was supported by Commissioner Eaton, and adopted. The committee on the
Rhode Island Schoolmaster reported its management to be
eminently satisfactory. The list of contributing editors
nominated, was elected. Messrs. Bicknell, Mowry and Hoyt
were appointed a committee to confer with other States in
reference to a New England school journal, and should any
plan be presented for establishing such a journal that the
matter be referred to the Board of Directors for action. A
committee was appointed to collect membership fees for the
Institute and take subscriptions for the *Schoolmaster*. The
officers of the Institute for the year ensuing were elected.
President Lyon declining a re-election, Mr. Isaac F. Cady
was unanimously chosen to succeed him. The customary
votes of thanks were passed. The printing of the History
of the Institute was referred to the Board of Directors. The
final hour of the session was devoted to the relation of educational reminiscences, by several of the early members.

President Lyon spoke of his earlier connection with the

Institute, and of those who were his co-laborers then. He alluded to the remark of Dr. Wayland that "Rhode Island ought to be the Attica of America." He expressed his pleasure at being here under such encouraging circumstances. We come back to the old homestead. The Institute has changed the character of the teaching in the State. Its great influence is shown by such a meeting as last evening. He spoke of the effect of silent forces, beautifully illustrating it by a certain remarkable ocean current. He closed his remarks with flattering allusions to his old friend and adviser, whom he introduced.

Hon. John Kingsbury then said:

I wish to welcome the old friends, and extend a cordial greeting to the younger and new ones. I believe in teaching from the call of the "*vox interna.*" My early experiences of injustice in school awakened in me a desire to teach. Discipline should be administered upon the strong and those of high position, as well as to others. Indeed, this is the most effective place to begin. He continued his remarks, giving some of his experience in regard to memorizing text-books. He believed that analytic study weakened the *word-memory,* making it difficult to commit verbatim.

President Lyon, alluding to Mr. Kingsbury as the first President of the Institute, now introduced the second, Prof. S. S. Greene, who said:

I have tried in vain to excuse myself from speaking. I recall, with great interest, my early connection with this work. I believe the Institute has been especially successful in disseminating methods of teaching throughout the State. I believe there has been great progress in methods within the last twenty years. I do not claim that we have all the best methods, or that we have settled methods, but there has been improvement. We have been experimenting sometimes with advantage, sometimes with disadvantage. This has been necessary; but if we have profited by experience, it has not been all loss. Geography is not now taught exclusively by text-books, but by maps and drawings. The modes of teaching arithmetic and spelling are in advance of those of twenty years ago. As regards committing to memory, the truth is, all lessons should be committed to memory, and should be understood. The power of language and expression should be cultivated. Language is the grand instrument by which we impress ourselves upon those around us. The motto of the teacher should be "Thought and expression, *both.*" There is yet much to be learned of teaching language. Thought is the matter, language the means of using it.

Hon. Amos Perry was introduced as a prominent mover in establishing the Institute. He related some interesting reminiscences of the organizing in 1844, alluding to the interest and success of Mr. Barnard in the work of education in Rhode Island at that time, when Horace Mann said, "To disperse a mob, announce an educational meeting." There was then great opposition to supporting public schools. Our success has been more than the warmest friends could have anticipated. Our re-union must be in part, of spirit, as some are no more present in the body. We treasure the memory of many. He spoke further of the changes in use of text-books which formerly were subject to the unanimous approval of the Grammar school teachers and thus made changes infrequent.

The historian of the Institute was now called upon :

He was reminded of the Jewish feasts when the tribes came up to Jerusalem, to rejoice over the ingathered harvest. So the teachers of our State, the faithful laborers in the wide domain of instruction, are here to-day to enjoy the recitals of educational progress, and in the prosperity with which the past has been crowned, to find incitements for the earnest work of the future. He alluded to the comprehensiveness and interest of subjects on the programme and to the independence of thought manifested in the papers and discussions. He approved of the increase of male teachers, but would not have fewer female teachers. We should have more teachers and smaller schools. He would have not more than thirty scholars under a single teacher. This would enable teachers to give a personal attention to each pupil, which, with a school of fifty, sixty or more is impossible. It would also insure thoroughness in the work of the school room, and though such a system might enhance the expense of maintaining schools, the compensation would be found in the more rapid progress of the scholars. Doubtless one-quarter, if not one-third, of the time now required for a full course of study could thus be saved. He referred to the effect of education as shown in the spirit of national arbitration. He thought education should reach the heart as well as the intellect.

It was a striking coincidence that this annual session of the Institute, distinguished for numbers, enthusiasm, and an af-

13

fluence of practical ideas, should have rounded up its one
hundredth meeting, and there was pertinancy in devoting its
last moments to an interchange of pleasant memories.

Normal School.

It will be seen by the preceding pages that a Normal
School, as a perfecting feature of our public school system,
appears not for a moment to have been lost sight of by the
friends of education. In and out of the Institute the need
of a school for the training of teachers, or in familiar phrase,
"to teach teachers how to teach," was freely discussed, and
earnestly recommended.

In 1850, a Didactic Department was established in Brown
University, designed to do the work of a Normal School,
and in 1851, Samuel S. Greene, Esq., then recently elected
Superintendent of Public Schools in Providence, was permitted by vote of the School Committee, to accept the Professorship of the same in connection with his duties due to
the city. But however gratifying were the fruits of this
arrangement, it soon became clear that to secure the best results of a Normal Institution,—to make its work reach further and accomplish more than the Didactic Department of
the University was able to do, it must be popularized, and to
popularize it, the Institution must stand in close relations
with the schools for which its labors were to be performed.

With this conviction, a Normal School was opened in Providence, October 24, 1852, as a private enterprise by Messrs.
Greene, Russell, Colburn and Guyot; and Mr. Greene
having resigned the Professorship of Didactics in the University, he was permitted by the School Committee to devote
a portion of his time to this school. During two sessions of
five months each it was attended by a large class of pupils
wishing to prepare themselves for teachers, and did much to
extend an interest in Normal instruction. But to give it the
assurance of permanency, Municipal or State sanction and
control were necessary.

At this juncture the School Committee of Providence took up the subject, looking to the establishing of such a school for its own teachers, and at a special meeting, December 20, 1853, a committee consisting of Theodore Cook, Edwin M. Stone, William Gammell, Amos D. Smith, and Gamaliel L. Dwight, was appointed to consider the plan, and report at a subsequent meeting. This they did January 13, 1854, and presented the following resolution, which was adopted :

Resolved, That in the opinion of this committee, the time has arrived when a Normal School for the education of teachers should be added to our system of public instruction, and that it be recommended to the City Council to establish such a school, either separately, for the exclusive benefit of the city, or in connection with the government of the State of Rhode Island, for the joint benefit of the city and the State, as in their wisdom they may deem best.

In accordance with this resolution, a code of rules and regulations was drawn up and adopted, and the Committee of Qualifications was authorized to open the school at such time as it should deem expedient. The City Council made the required appropriation, and everything seemed in readiness for continuing the school on a new basis. This movement of the city may have hastened the action of the State, for, at the May session of the General Assembly, an act was passed, establishing a State Normal School, and $3,000 were appropriated for its support. Although the city left the field to be occupied exclusively by the State, the School Committee showed its cordial approval of what had been done, by authorising Professor Greene to give a daily lecture to the school on the English language, and on the government and organization of the different grades of schools, for which service he was allowed to receive such compensation as might be agreed upon between himself and the State authorities.

On the 29th of May, the school was inaugurated with appropriate ceremonies, in the presence of Governor Hoppin and a large assemblage of the friends of the Institution. An earnest congratulatory address was made by the Governor. The inaugural address was delivered by Commissioner Potter. In this, he treated of the province of a Normal School, what might and what might not be rightly expected of it. He spoke of the difficulties it would have to contend with, and touched upon manners as an essential feature of the school room, and of moral instruction as a vital element in the system of education.

Thus, after nine years of anxious waiting on the part of the Institute for the germination of the seed thought sown by Mr. Barnard, the Normal School came into being, to fill an unoccupied place, and to elevate the standard of teaching qualifications. Of this school Mr. Dana P. Colburn was appointed Principal, and Mr. Arthur Sumner, Assistant, the former at an annual salary of $1,200, and the latter at $750.

The school was continued in Providence with flattering success until 1857, when it was removed to Bristol. After the lamented death of Mr. Colburn,* Mr. Joshua Kendall, of Meadville, Pa., was appointed Principal. Mr. Kendall

---

*Dana Pond Colburn the youngest of a family of fifteen children, was a son of Isaacus Colburn, and was born in West Dedham, Mass., September 24th, 1823. After suitable preparation he entered the Normal School, at Bridgewater, Mass., in the spring of 1843, for the purpose of qualifying himself to become a teacher. Having completed his course of study in that institution, he commenced school teaching in the town of Dover, and afterwards taught in Sharon, then in East Greenwich, R. I., and subsequently in Brookline, Mass. In 1847 he was employed by Horace Mann, Secretary of the Massachusetts Board of Education, to conduct Teachers' Institutes. In the following year, Rev. Dr. Sears, Mr. Mann's successor, re-engaged him as one of the corps of Institute instructors. In 1848 he became an assistant teacher in the Normal School at Bridgewater, and in 1850, removed to Newton, to engage in private tuition, and to assist Dr. Sears in conducting Institutes. In 1852, as already mentioned, he commenced Normal Instruction in Providence, and remained at the head of the state Institution until December 15th, 1859, on which day he was suddenly killed in Bristol. He was thrown from his carriage while taking his customary afternoon ride, dragged a considerable distance over the frozen ground, and was taken up fearfully mangled and lifeless. His remains were removed for burial to his native town. He was the author of several arithmetics, which obtained a good reputation among teachers. Mr. Colburn was, at the time of his death, in the 47th year of his age. "Thus early perished one whose qualities of mind and heart made him admired and loved by all who knew him."

brought to his new and somewhat difficult position a thoroughly trained mind, scholarly attainments, a high ideal of intellectual and moral culture, and an ardent devotion to his work. His services were justly appreciated by the Board of Trustees, who gave him their hearty co operation. He continued in the successful discharge of his duties until April, 1864, when he resigned and removed to Cambridge, Mass.*

The school was continued upwards of a year after Mr. Kendall's resignation, under the charge of a female Principal, but the location having proved unfavorable to its continued prosperity, it was suspended July 3, 1865. For a number of years various plans for resuscitating it were devised, but without effect. But after a suspension of more than six years, a more favorable condition of the public mind prevailed. The school was re-established by the General Assembly, at the January session, 1871, and was opened September 6th, the same year, in Normal Hall, formerly the High Street Congregational Church, in the city of Providence, with impressive services. Governor Padelford delivered the inaugural address, in the presence of an audience that filled the Hall to its full capacity. Of the school thus revived, J. C. Greenough, A. B., an instructor of experience from the Normal School at Westfield, Mass., was appointed Principal. The school opened with a large accession of pupils, and has since continued in a highly prosperous condition.†

* The female assistants in the school from 1860 to 1865 were Misses Harriet Goodwin, Ellen R. Luther, and Ellen G. LeGro. In 1861, Mr. Loomis was employed to give instruction in vocal music.

† Mr. Greenough's assistants are, (November, 1874,) Misses Susan C. Bancroft, Mary L. Jewett, Sarah Marble, and Anna C. Bucklin. The school year of this Institution is divided into two terms of twenty-one weeks each, including a recess of one week in the Spring and Summer term, and the same in the Fall and Winter term. In the latter an additional recess of three days during Thanksgiving week is taken. The course of lectures and special instruction comprises Moral Science, Language, Mediæval and English History, Physiology, Mathematics, Rhetoric, School Laws of Rhode Island, French, Elocution, Drawing, Penmanship and German.

From the opening in September, 1871, to September, 1874, 328 pupils have been registered and 104 have graduated.

Evening Schools.

The first evening free school in Rhode Island was opened in Providence in 1842, under the auspices of the Ministry-at-Large, to meet a class of wants then existing, which were not supplied by the day schools. For thirteen years it was continued with gratifying success. In the meantime public attention had been attracted to this class of schools, a sympathy for them was created, and in 1849 two were opened by the School Committee of Providence. In subsequent years they have increased as the needs of the community demanded. They are open to adults and are numerously attended by young persons older than the average age of pupils in the Grammar Schools. The number of pupils enrolled for the winter session of 1873–74, was 2,566, and the improvement in the several branches taught showed a commendable studiousness. Evening schools have been, for many years, embraced in the school system of Providence, and are regarded with universal favor.

Mr. Barnard, in his report to the General Assembly in 1845, recommended opening evening schools "for apprentices, clerks, and other young persons," who had been hurried into active employment without a suitable elementary education, and he thought it was not beyond the legitimate scope of a system of public instruction to provide in this way for the education of adults, who, from any cause, had been deprived of the advantages of school instruction. The Institute, too, has at different times, as already seen, recognized the value of evening schools by emphatic votes of commendation.

In 1868, in view of the increase in the State by immigration of an uneducated population, a number of gentlemen, manufacturers and others, organized an association known as "*The Rhode Island Educational Union*," for the purpose of establishing, wherever possible, evening schools, reading rooms, and other means of intellectual improvement for the classes before referred to. Mr. Samuel Austin, of Providence, an experienced educator, with many years' experience in conducting schools of this description, was appointed General Agent of the *Union*. In this capacity he visited different parts of the State to awaken an interest in their behalf. His labors have proved very successful. In the winter of 1873–74, upwards of sixty evening schools were in operation, affording educational advantages which were availed of by more than six thousand persons.

At a convention of the school officers of the State, called by the Commissioner of Public Schools, and held in Providence, January 13, 1871, evening schools were among the important topics presented for consideration. Since then the Board of Education has sanctioned them, and secured from the General Assembly liberal grants for their encouragement. In his annual report for 1871, the State Commissioner made evening schools a prominent feature, and in 1873 he reports that they continue to furnish to a large number of persons " advantages for study, of which they were deprived in earlier years, and the value of which they have learned practically by experiencing their loss." Evening schools are not intended to rival, supplant, or in any way weaken the efficiency of the day schools, but to supplement them by providing the means of education for the classes already named, who are beyond the reach of other methods.

Wisely conducted, schools of this character, in a manufacturing State like Rhode Island, will prove " a beneficent agency for securing the end desired," viz. : the diffusion of intelligence, and the development of a higher moral and social condition among the great body of the people.

Conclusion.

In the preceding pages the names of many of the founders of the RHODE ISLAND INSTITUTE OF INSTRUCTION have appeared, and their persistent labors amidst numerous discouragements to advance the cause of education throughout the

State have found an honorable record. Yet while all wrought well and deserve the meed of praise, it will not be invidious to repeat the names of some of the number, to whom, more than to all others, the Institute was indebted for its early prosperity. On this high record will ever stand conspicuous the names of Francis Wayland,* John Kingsbury, John L.

*From the very beginning, the Institute and the cause of popular education found an earnest, steadfast and strong supporter in President Wayland. He correctly appreciated the importance of so fostering and improving the common schools of the State, that a parent, to use his own words, "need look nowhere else for as good instruction as his family may require," and that gauged by this standard, "public instruction should be provided in sufficient extent to meet the wants of the community."—(Report to Providence School Committee, April 22, 1828.)

He advocated a High School as a part of our system of public instruction,—"a school which should provide instruction in all that is necessary for a finished education."

In the realm of mind, Dr. Wayland repudiated the factitious distinctions of caste. For the Fergusons, Paxtons, Millers, Franklins, Fultons, Rittenhouses, Whitneys, Bowditches, Chases, Wilsons, and Greeleys, of however humble origin, he would have provided the most favorable opportunities for the full development of their intellectual powers; and he believed that bringing all classes into our public schools, to pursue together the studies that were to qualify them for literary or business life, was not only a consistent illustration of the spirit of our free institutions, but a pledge of their perpetuity.

Acting under this conviction, his time and labor were freely given to secure these high results. Every call for words of counsel or of encouragement was promptly and cheerfully answered, and his services in aid of the President of the Institute, while conducting educational meetings in various towns of the State, as well as in other ways, were invaluable. The key note of his thought at this period found expression in these words: "Cultivate enlarged and liberal views of your duties to the young, who are coming after you, and of the means that are given you to discharge them. . . . Your example would excite others to follow in your footsteps. Who can tell how widely you might bless others, while you were laboring to bless yourselves."—(Address at Pawtucket, October 31, 1846.)

For many years Dr. Wayland was an active and influential member of the School Committee in Providence. In 1828, when the school system of that city was re-organized, he, as chairman of a committee to whom the whole subject had been referred, drew up an elaborate and exhaustive report, which led to the adoption of several important changes. As an educator in the higher departments of learning, he ranked with the foremost of his time, while his interest in the Public Free School system, and in the work of the INSTITUTE, continued unabated to the

Hughes, Wilkins Updike, Thomas Shepard,* Elisha R. Potter, Sylvester G. Shearman, Henry A. Dumont, Lemuel H. Arnold, Isaac Hall, George W. Cross, Horace Babcock, Christopher C. Greene, William Gammell, Silas R. Kenyon, R. G. Burlingame, Nathan Bishop, John J. Stimson, Amos Perry, Thomas C. Hartshorn, William T. Grinnell, Samuel Austin, William D. Brayton, Sylvester Patterson, Thomas Waterman, Thomas R. Hazard, Joshua D. Giddings, Rowland G. Hazard, Moses Brown Ives,† George Manchester, Christopher G. Perry, Jesse S. Tourtellot, Jenckes Mowry, John J. Kilton, Joseph T. Sisson, Latimer Ballou, Samuel

close of life. His name will ever be identified with the history of education and philanthropy in Rhode Island.

Dr. Wayland presided over Brown University from 1827 to 1855, and subsequently was two years a member of the Corporation. He died September 26, 1865.

*For nearly or quite half a century, Rev. Dr. Shepard, of Bristol, has participated in important movements in behalf of public education in this State. As a member of the School Committee of the town, and for a series of years its chairman, and as a trustee of the first State Normal School, he has rendered valuable services to the cause. For many years he was an officer of the RHODE ISLAND INSTITUTE OF INSTRUCTION, and its meetings were often made more effective by the part he took in its deliberations. Dr. Shepard still lives, at an advanced age, to derive pleasure from a contemplation of the progress of a work which he has done so much to promote.

†In an address before the Institute in 1873, Hon. John Kingsbury related the following incident, honorable to the public spirit of Mr. Ives. It occurred in 1828, when "there was a formidable opposition to the proposed improvement of our schools," even in the school committee. "In this committee there was one of our merchant princes. He was a man of great modesty, of deeds rather than words. In the discussion, which was warm and protracted, he had taken no part. Just as the question was about to be taken, he arose, and said substantially: 'Mr. Chairman, I have heard the arguments on this subject with careful attention, and am ready to give my vote. I prefer to leave my children less money in a community well educated, rather than a greater amount in a community imperfectly educated; I shall vote in the affirmative on the question.' These words, though few, fell with crushing weight upon the opposition, and the school ordinance was adopted. This was the late Moses Brown Ives, a man whose purse was always ready to sustain his vote on this occasion. From this fact it is easy to infer that the attempt to enlist property holders, especially rich men, against the improvement of our public schools, was a decided failure."

14

Greene, Caleb Farnum, Christopher T. Keith, George C.
Wilson, Elisha S. Baggs, John B. Tallman, Ariel Ballou,
John Boyden,* Thomas Vernon, O. F. Otis, Thomas S. Vail,
George A. Willard, and Edward B. Hall. Many of these
gentlemen, as well as others not named, were practical educators ; some of them occupied influential positions of political trust, and all of them were ardently devoted to the objects
of the Institute. They and their associates were pioneers in
a cause that held out few popular inducements to become its
advocates. Indeed, in many instances, personal popularity
was jeopardized by their zealous devotion to a work which
conflicted at once with prejudiced and contracted ideas of private and public duty. But they rose above the low ambitions
of mere politicians. They kept before them the one great
purpose of shedding the blessings of education upon the
entire State, and employed every judicious agency at command to carry forward their plans to completion. While
some of their number have passed on to higher scenes, without witnessing the consummation of their desires, others of
them still live to rejoice in a radical revolution of public
opinion and practice, and especially in the commanding position our public schools now occupy in the hearts of the peo-

* Rev. John Boyden was born in Sturbridge, Mass., May 14th, 1809. An experience in school teaching doubtless laid the foundation for the interest he subsequently manifested in the cause of education. He selected the Christian ministry
for his profession, studied divinity with Rev. Hosea Ballou, of Boston, and was
settled, successively, at Berlin, and Dudley, Mass., and Woonsocket, R. I. To the
latter place he removed in 1840, and became pastor of the Universalist Society.
For many years he had charge of the public schools of Cumberland, as visiting
and examining committee. He was an original member of the RHODE ISLAND
INSTITUTE OF INSTRUCTION, and did much to promote its early prosperity. After
the Normal School was established, he was chosen one of its trustees, and dis-
charged the duties of his office with scrupulous fidelity. As a citizen, Mr. Boyden
was highly respected, and at different periods was chosen to bear Representative
and Senatorial honors in the General Assembly of Rhode Island. He possessed a
fine musical taste, and was the author of a Sunday school singing book. He died
of pulmonary disease, September 28, 1869, in the 61st year of his age, widely and
deeply lamented.

ple. The value of their unselfish labors, at a time when there was so much to be done and so few to do it, is beyond estimate. The advantages that those labors have already secured, and will perpetuate to future generations, cannot be mathematically determined. But when riches shall have become corrupted, and the gold and silver of selfish enterprise shall be cankered, and the rust thereof shall be a witness against its possessors, the memory of those who scattered broadcast the seeds of good knowledge, and laid the foundation of a generous culture, embracing without distinction the young of every rank, will impart fragrance to the true glory of the State.

In reviewing the work of the Institute, its members may justly feel that there is cause for congratulation. A glance at the summary of one hundred meetings, held in various parts of the State, will show that the Institute not only commenced its labors with the advocacy of a *Normal School*, but has led public opinion in every movement originated for the improvement of our public school system. It early encouraged the formation of *Town* and *District Libraries*, the introduction of *Music* into the public schools as an important element of culture, the establishing of a *Board of Education*, "by the aid of which the Public Schools would be safe from the influences of politics and the evils of sectarian prejudices," and the opening of *Evening Schools* in our manufacturing villages, to meet an imperative want of the operative population.

It will also be noticed that the list of lecturers comprises many of the ablest educators in our country. It will likewise be seen that the range of topics considered at these meetings evinced a breadth of view not elsewhere surpassed, and touching every point vital to the advancement of our schools.

A great work for Rhode Island has been done, and well done. For the encouraging results everywhere visible, much is due to the labors of a succession of able State Commissioners, much to the General Assembly for its liberal appropriations in aid of Institute meetings, for increasing the circulation of the *Rhode Island Schoolmaster*, for the support of the Normal School, and for the encouragement of Evening Schools. A great work has been done by the Institute, by the Normal School, by the Board of Education, by earnest teachers, by faithful town and city school superintendents, and by no less faithful school committees. For all this the friends of education may thank God and take courage.

But while a commendable pride may be indulged in view of the success of the past, it is by no means to be assumed that the mission of this Institution has been consummated, and that having witnessed an educational millennium, it may rest on its laurels, or disband as having no field for further service. The millennium is not yet come. There is still darkness to be dispersed. Low ideas of intellectual culture remain to be raised, by the force of intelligence, to a higher plane. The hygiene of the school-room is yet to be better understood. Teaching, as an art, admits of further improvement. The importance of moral instruction, its character and place, in our schools, is a question still demanding profound consideration, and the responsibilities of parents and of the State in securing to every child of suitable years a good practical education need yet to be made more plain and enforced with increased vigor. While man continues a progressive being, and each succeeding generation shows characteristics peculiarly its own, the methods of instruction must so far change as to answer the needs of the changed condition of society. The day, therefore, is far off in which the RHODE ISLAND INSTITUTE OF INSTRUCTION can feel authorized to withdraw from the scenes of its past action and lay aside its armor. It will still work on, and by wise measures aid in carrying forward to its highest success the cause to which for thirty years it has been unweariedly devoted.

In closing this outline of history, there is appropriateness in reaffirming the sentiments held by the Institute at its organization, and expressed by its Executive Committee in its first annual report :

" The importance of the education of the people—the object for which this Association was formed—cannot be estimated too highly. By the side of it most other public interests appear small and transitory. This stands out before every other, and challenges the attention and the efforts of all who would advance the present prosperity, or the future fortunes of the State. To train the rising generation to knowledge and virtue, to raise up intelligent and true-hearted citizens, who shall understand their rights and their duties, and shall guard the honor and the interests of society—these have always been regarded as the highest ends which enlightened policy can aim to accomplish. But great and important as these objects are to every community, they assume a still greater importance to us as citizens of Rhode Island. Our prosperity and progress as a Sovereign State—our position and our influence as members of this growing confederacy of republics, must depend. not upon the extent of our territory, the number of our population, or the natural wealth of our soil, but upon the character of our citizens. It is this alone which can give us a voice in the councils of the nation, and a worthy name and place among the States of the Union. Our aim should therefore be, to be strong in high-minded, heroic men. These constitute a State; without them, no advantages of nature, no monuments of art, no battlements of physical force, no achievements of manufacturing or agricultural industry, will be able to maintain its honor, or perpetuate its renown."

APPENDIX.

CONSTITUTION.

ADOPTED AT A PUBLIC MEETING OF THE FRIENDS OF POPULAR EDU-
CATION FROM ALL PARTS OF THE STATE, AT WESTMINSTER
HALL, PROVIDENCE, JANUARY 24, 1845.

ARTICLE 1. This association shall be styled the " RHODE ISLAND IN-
STITUTE OF INSTRUCTION," and shall have for its object the improve-
ment of public schools, and other means of popular education in this
State.

ARTICLE 2. Any person residing in this State may become a member
of the Institute by subscribing to this Constitution, (and contributing any
sum towards defraying its incidental expenses.)*

ARTICLE 3. The Officers of the Institute shall be a President, two or
more Vice Presidents, a Recording Secretary, a Corresponding Secretary,
a Treasurer, (with such powers and duties, respectively, as their several
designations imply,) and Directors, who shall together constitute an
Executive Committee.

* January 19, 1853, the Constitution was so amended as to allow persons to become members of the Institute without the payment of any fee. January 18,
1872, it was voted that an annual tax of one dollar should be assessed on male
members, and fifty cents on female members of the Institute.

ARTICLE 4. The Executive Committee shall carry into effect such measures as the Institute may direct; and for this purpose, and to promote the general object of the Institute, may appoint special committees, collect and disseminate information, call public meetings for lectures and discussions, circulate books, periodicals and pamphlets on the subject of schools, school systems, and education generally, and perform such other acts as they may deem necessary or expedient, and make report of their doings to the Institute at its annual meeting.

ARTICLE 5. A meeting of the Institute for the choice of Officers shall be held annually in the city of Providence, in the month of January, at such time and place as the Executive Committee may designate, in a notice published in one or more of the city papers; and meetings may be held at such other times and places as the Executive Committee may appoint.

ARTICLE 6. This Constitution may be altered (or amended) at any annual meeting, by a majority of the members present, and any regulations not inconsistent with its provisions may be adopted at any meeting.

CHARTER.

STATE OF RHODE ISLAND, IN GENERAL ASSEMBLY,
JANUARY SESSION, A. D. 1863.

AN ACT TO INCORPORATE THE RHODE ISLAND INSTITUTE OF
INSTRUCTION.

It is enacted by the General Assembly as follows:

SECTION 1.   Francis Wayland, Alexis Caswell, Moses B. Lockwood, Amos Perry, James Y. Smith, Shubael Hutchins, John Kingsbury, Samuel S. Greene, E. M. Stone, A. W. Godding, C. T. Keith, A. A. Gamwell, John Boyden, Daniel Leach, Emory Lyon, George A. Willard, B. V. Gallup, William A. Mowry. Alexander Duncan, S. A. Potter, Joshua Kendall. Henry Rousmaniere, J. T. Edwards, J. H. Tefft, M. S. Greene, W. B. Cook, I. F. Cady. Samuel Austin, A. J. Manchester, J. J. Ladd, N. W. DeMunn, F. B. Snow, Thomas Davis, A. C. Robbins, D. R. Adams, Joseph Eastman. H. M. Rice, T. W. Bicknell, Samuel Thurber, H. N. Slater, Edward Harris, A. J. Foster, J. M. Ross, F. J. Belden, Thomas Shepard, E. R. Potter, J. B. Chapin, and such others as now are, or hereafter may be, associated with them, be, and they are hereby constituted, created and made a body politic and corporate with perpetual succession, by the name and style of "THE RHODE ISLAND INSTITUTE OF INSTRUCTION," with full powers to make and ordain, alter and amend, such by-laws and regulations for their government, as they may think necessary, the same not being contrary to the laws of the State; and they are empowered by the aforesaid name, to sue and be sued, to plead and be impleaded, to hold and enjoy any kind of real or personal

15

estate, to an amount not exceeding ten thousand dollars, whether obtained by gift, demise, purchase, or otherwise, and to dispose of and convey the same at pleasure, to have and use a common seal, which they may alter or change as they may think proper.

Sec. 2. The officers elected under the following Constitution, or who may be elected in accordance with its provisions, shall be the officers of the Institute until the next annual meeting, and until others are elected in their places, and the following shall be the Constitution of the Institute, until it shall be duly altered or amended as is therein provided.*

I certify the foregoing to be a true copy.

In testimony whereof, I have hereunto set my hand and affixed the seal of the State, this eighteenth day of November, A D. 1872.

JOSHUA M. ADDEMAN,

Secretary of State.

* For copy of Constitution see two preceding pages.

RHODE ISLAND SCHOOLMASTER, PAGE 95.

In November, 1871, arrangements were made to merge the *Schoolmaster*, the *Massachusetts Teacher*, the *Maine Journal of Education*, and the *Connecticut School Journal*, into one paper, quarto form, of sixteen pages, to be called *The New England Journal of Education*. Its editor will be Hon. Thomas W. Bicknell. Mr. David W. Hoyt, Principal of the English and Scientific Department of the Providence High School, represents Rhode Island as Counsellor on the Board of Directors. The *Journal* will have a local department for Rhode Island, of which Mr. Thomas B. Stockwell, of the Classical Department, Providence High School, will be editor.

OFFICERS OF THE INSTITUTE

PRESIDENTS.

John Kingsbury,	- - - -	1845 to 1856.
Samuel S. Greene,	- - - -	1856 to 1860.
John J. Ladd,	- - - -	1860 to 1864.
William A. Mowry,	- ; - -	1864 to 1866.
Thomas W. Bicknell.	- - - -	1866 to 1868.
Noble W. DeMunn,	- - - -	1868 to 1869.
James T. Edwards,	- - - -	1869 to 1870.
Albert J. Manchester,	- - - -	1870 to 1872.
Merrick Lyon,	- - - -	1872 to 1874.
Isaac F. Cady.	- - - -	1874 to

VICE PRESIDENTS.

*Wilkins Updike,	- - - -	1845 to 1847.
Ariel Ballou,	- - - -	1845 to 1850.
C. G. Perry, -	- - -	1846 to 1848.
Thomas Shepard,	- - - -	1846 to 1860.
John J. Kilton.	- - - -	1846 to 1850.
Elisha R. Potter, Jr.	- - - -	1847 to 1860.
Jesse S. Tourtellot.	- - - -	1847 to 1848.
*A. H. Dumont,	- - - -	1848 to 1866.
J. W. Cooke, -	- - - -	1848 to 1850.
*John Boyden, Jr., -	- - - -	1850 to 1870.
*Elisha Harris,	- - - -	1850 to 1860.
Robert Allyn,	- - - -	1855 to 1858.
T. H. Vail, -	- - - -	1856 to 1858.
*S. A. Crane.	- - - -	1856 to 1860
Thomas R. Hazard,	- - - -	1857 to 1860.
John Kingsbury, -	- - - -	1858 to 1860.
*Albert A. Gamwell,	- - - -	1860 to 1872.
William A. Mowry,	- 1860 to 1861.—1862 to 1864.—1868 to 1870.	

Samuel Austin,	-	-	-	1860 to 1868.—1872 to 1873.
Isaac F. Cady,	1860 to 1862.—1864 to 1866.—1868 to 1871.—1872 to 1874.			
Joshua Kendall.	-	-	-	1861 to 1865.
Noble W. DeMunn.	-	-	1861 to 1862.—1870 to 1871.	
*Henry R. Pierce,	-	-	-	1861 to 1862.
George A. Willard,	-	-	-	1861 to 1868.
Benjamin V. Gallup,	-	1861 to 1862.—1864 to 1865.—1866 to 1868.		
J. H. Tefft,	-	-	-	1862 to 1873.
Dwight R. Adams,	-	-	-	1863 to 1870.
James M. Ross,	-	-	-	1864 to 1867.
Benjamin F. Hayes,	-	-	-	1864 to 1866.
Benjamin F. Clarke,	-	-	-	-
David W. Hoyt,	-	-	1865 to 1871.—1872 to
Charles B. Goff,	-	-	-	1865 to 1868.
Thomas W. Bicknell,	-	-	1865 to 1866.—1870 to
Samuel Thurber,	-	-	-	1865 to 1866.
Henry S. Latham,	-	-	-	1865 to 1868.
Joshua B. Chapin,	-	-	-	1866 to 1871.
John J. Ladd,	-	-	1866 to 1867.—1869 to 1870.	
Edwin M. Stone,	-	-	1866 to 1871.—1872 to
M. J. Talbot,	-	-	-	1866 to 1867.
James T. Edwards,	-	-	-	1866 to 1869.
William H. Bowen,	-	-	-	1866 to 1868.
H. S. Shearman,	-	-	-	-
G. B. Inman,	-	-	-	1866 to 1868.
Daniel Leach,	-	-	-	1867 to
Samuel S. Greene,	-	-	-	1867 to 1870
A. Sherman,	-	-	-	1867 to 1868.
M. A. Aldrich.	-	-	-	1867 to 1869.
J. W. R. Marsh,	-	-	-	1867 to 1869.
H. W. Clarke,	-	-	-	1867 to 1874.
W. E. Tolman,	-	-	-	1867 to 1871.
P. E. Tillinghast,	-	-	-	1867 to 1868.
F. W. Tilton,	-	-	1868 to 1872.—1874 to
W. W. Warner,	-	-	-	1868 to 1870.
Levi W. Russell,	-	-	1869 to 1871.—1872 to
James M. Sawin,	-	-	-	1869 to 1871.
T H. Clarke,	-	-	1869 to 1871.—1873 to
Albert J. Manchester,	-	-	-	1870 to 1871.
Merrick Lyon,	-	-	-	1870 to 1872.
J. C. Stockbridge,	-	-	-	1870 to 1873.
Thomas B. Stockwell,	-	-	-	1870 to
E. K. Parker,	-	-	-	1870 to 1874.
G. F Whittemore,	-	-	-	1871 to 1872.
P. E. Bishop,	-	-	-	1871 to 1872.
J. S. Eastman,	-	-	-	1871 to
J. C. Greenough,	-	-	-	1872 to

A. D. Small.	-	-	-	-	1872 to 1874.
J. Milton Hall,	-	-	-		1872 to
Sarah E. Doyle,	-	-	-	-	1872 to 1874.
M. E. Morse,	-	-	-	-	1872 to 1873.
O. P. Fuller,	-	-	-	-	1872 to 1873.
Sarah Dean,	-	-	-	-	1872 to
Lizzie Brown,	-	-	-	-	1873 to 1874.
Edwin H. King,	-	-	-	-	1873 to 1871.
Benoni Carpenter,	-	-	-	-	1873 to 1874.
N. W. Littlefield,	-	-	-	-	1873 to
R. S. Andrews,	-	-	-	-	1873 to
Ira O Seamans,	-	-	-		1873 to 1874.
F. W. Wing,	-	-	-	-	1874 to
Ellen M. Haskell,	-	-	-	-	1874 to
H. M. Hunt,	-	-	-	-	1874 to
Lysander Flagg,	-	-	-	-	1874 to
Julia Lefavour,	-	-	-	-	1874 to
J. M. Brewster,	-	-	-	-	1874 to

CORRESPONDING SECRETARIES.

Nathan Bishop,	-	-	-	-	1845 to 1848.
Amos Perry,	-	-	-	-	1848 to 1851.
Zwinglius Grover,	-	-	-	1851 to 1855.—1856 to 1858.
Alvah W. Godding,	-	-	-	-	1858 to 1865.
Albert J. Manchester,	-	-	-	-	1865 to 1870.
Dwight R. Adams,	-	-	-	-	1870 to 1874.
Eli H. Howard,	-	-	-	-	1874 to

TREASURERS.

Thomas C. Hartshorn,	-	-	-	-	1845 to 1852.
Amos Perry,	-	-	-	-	1853 to 1856.
Christopher T. Keith,	-	-	-	-	1856 to 1862.
Noble W. DeMunn,	-	-	-	-	1862 to 1868.
B. V. Gallup,	-	-	-	-	1868 to

RECORDING SECRETARIES.

Joshua D. Giddings,	-	-	-	-	1845 to 1848.
Christopher T. Keith,	-	-	-	-	1848 to 1850.
Caleb Farnum,	-	-	-	-	1850 to 1851.
Albert A Gamwell,	-	-	-	-	1851 to 1854.
Alvah W. Godding,	-	-	-	-	1854 to 1858.
Edward H. Magill,	-	-	-	-	1858 to 1860.
Francis B. Snow,	-	-	-	-	1860 to 1862.
Alvin C. Robbins,	-	-	-	-	1862 to 1866.
Thomas B. Stockwell,	-	-	-	-	1866 to 1870.
J. E. Parker,	-	-	-	-	1870 to 1871.
Frank G. Morley,	-	-	-	-	1871 to 1872.

G. E. Whittemore,	-	-	-	-	1872 to 1874.
Lester A. Freeman,	-	-	-	-	1874 to

DIRECTORS.

William Gammell,	-	-	-	-	1845 to 1860.
James T. Sisson,	-	-	-	1845 to 1848.—1854 to 1855.
John B. Tallman, -	-		-	-	1845 to 1848.
Latimer W. Ballou,	-	-	-	-	1845 to 1846.
Samuel S. Greene,	-	-	-	1845 to 1848.—1852 to 1856.
James T. Harkness,	-	-	-	-	1845 to 1846.
Jesse S. Tourtellot,	-	-	-	1845 to 1847.—1848 to 1855.
Amos Perry, -	-	-	-	1845 to 1848.—1858 to 1862.
Caleb Farnum,	-	-	-	-	1845 to 1850.
George C. Wilson,	-	-	-	-	1846 to 1857.
William S. Baker, -	-	-	-	-	1846 to 1850.
Thomas R. Hazard,	-	-	-	-	1846 to 1856.
*John Boyden, Jr.,	-	-	1847 to 1848.—1856 to 1858.
Nathan Bishop,	-	-	-	-	1848 to 1852.
Thomas H. Vail, -	-	-	-	-	1848 to 1857.
Sylvester Patterson,	-	-	-	-	1848 to 1860.
Samuel Austin,	-	-	-	-	1848 to 1860.
C. G. Perry, -	-	-	-	-	1848 to 1855.
J. Bushee,	-	-	-	-	1848 to 1855.
Thomas Shepard,	-	-	-	-	1848 to 1850.
*Albert A. Gamwell,	-	-	-	-	1854 to 1860.
George W. Quereau,	-	-	-	-	1855 to 1860.
George A. Willard, -	-	-	-	-	1855 to 1860.
Edmund Gray, Jr.,	-	-	-	-	1855 to 1858.
Nathaniel B. Cooke,	-	-	-	-	1855 to 1861.
*John H. Willard,	-	-	-	-	1855 to 1860.
Orin F. Otis,	-	-	-	-	1855 to 1860.
*Dana P. Colburn,	-	-	-	-	1855 to 1860.
William H. Farrar,	-	-	-	-	1855 to 1857.
John Kingsbury,	-	-	-	-	1856 to 1858.
Daniel Leach,	-	-	-	-	1856 to 1860.
Edward H. Magill,	-	-	-	-	1856 to 1858.
Thomas G. Potter,	-	-	-	-	1856 to 1860.
C. C. Beaman,	-	-	-	-	1857 to 1858.
Edwin M. Stone, -	-	-	-	-	1857 to 1866.
E. Grant,	-	-	-	-	1857 to 1858.
Lucius A. Wheelock,	-	-	-	-	1858 to 1860.
Charles Hutchins,	-	-	-	-	1858 to 1859.
William G. Crosby,	-	-	-	-	1858 to 1860.
J. B. Breed, -	-	-	-	-	1858 to 1860.
Merrick Lyon,	-	-	-	1858 to 1869.—1874 to
Albert J. Manchester, -	-	-	-	1860 to 1862.—1872 to

Millen S. Greene, - - - - -	1860 to 1866.
William A. Mowry, - - -	1861 to 1862.—1866 to
Isaac F. Cady, - - - - -	1862 to 1870.
Joseph S. Eastman, - - - -	1861 to 1866.
Howard M. Rice, - - - - -	1862 to 1864.
Francis B. Snow, - - - -	1862 to 1867.
Thomas Davis, - - - - -	1862 to 1866.
James T. Edwards, - - - -	1863 to 1865.
Thomas W. Bicknell, - -	1863 to 1866.—1868 to 1869.
Alvan C. Robbins, - - - -	1866 to
J. M. Collins, - - - - -	1866 to 1867.
Benjamin F. Clarke, - - - -	1866 to 1868.
W. E. Woodbridge, - - - -	1867 to 1868.
Frederic W. Tilton, - - - -	1868 to 1870.
Dwight R. Adams, - - -	1868 to 1870 —1874 to
J. R Davenport, - - - -	1870 to 1872.
J. Q. Adams, - - - - -	1870 to 1874.
H. W. Clarke, - - -	1870 to 1871.—1874 to
F. G. Morley, - -	1870 to 1871.—1872 to
J. T. Durfee, - - - - -	1870 to 1874.
L. C. Greene, - - - - -	1870 to 1871.
T. H. Clarke, - - - -	1871 to 1872.
*Osceola H. Kile, - - - -	1871 to 1874.
A. J. Lincoln, - - - -	1871 to 1872.
W. E. Tolman, - - - -	1871 to
E. H. Howard, - - - -	1871 to 1874.
Sarah E Doyle, - - - -	1872 to
H. A. Benson, - - - -	1872 to
A. G. Chace, - - - - -	1872 to 1873.
Mary A. Riley, - - - - -	1873 to
William A. Phillips, - - - -	1873 to 1874.
George W. Cole, - - - -	1873 to
Susan C Bancroft, - - - -	1874 to
Emory Lyon, - - - - -	1874 to
Alonzo Williams, - - - -	1874 to
Mrs. G. E. Whittemore, - - -	1874 to
Mrs C. Barker, - - - -	1874 to
Henry A. Wood, - - - -	1874 to
T. D. Blakeslie, - - - -	1874 to
Stephen C. Irons, - - - -	1874 to

LIST OF MEMBERS

[EXPLANATION.—The names of the founders of the INSTITUTE, so far as ascertained, are suffixed with a †. An asterisk (*) is prefixed to the names of deceased members. Probably the Necrology is much larger than indicated by the sign. The location of each teacher is that given in signing the Constitution. Possibly errors in christian names may have occurred. If any such are discovered, the author will be grateful for the information.]

Allen, Zachariah†	Providence,	Previous to 1872.
*Adams, Seth Jr.†	"	" "
Aborn, Joseph†	"	" "
Austin, Samuel†	"	" "
*Atwater, Stephen†	"	" "
Aldrich, Harris W. (1849.)	"	" "
Austin, Sarah	"	" "
Andrews, Caroline F.	"	" "
Allen, Christopher†	North Providence,	" "
Adams, Dwight R.	Centreville,	" "
Aldrich, Mary J.	Slatersville,	" "
Allyn, Robert Rev.	East Greenwich,	" "
Allen, Hiram	Woonsocket,	" "
Angell, Nehemiah A.	North Scituate,	" "
Arnold, S. B	Woonsocket,	" "
Almy, Peleg	Tiverton,	" "
Allen, Sarah	Woonsocket,	" "
Andrews, R. S.	Bristol,	" "
Arnold, Rufus,	Woonsocket,	" "
Allen, Edward A. H.	New Bedford, Mass.,	" "
Anthony, Joseph (1849)	Newport,	" "
Aldrich, Melda	Cumberland,	" "
Aldrich, Wilmarth N.†	Providence,	" "
Adams, J. Q.	Natick,	" "

Arnold, M. W.†	Providence,	Previous to 1872.
Ames, John.†	"	" "
Aldrich, Rebecca	Slatersville,	" "
Angell, Nancy W.	Pascoag,	" "
Allen, Charles L.	Tiverton,	" "
Adams. Ellie	Bristol,	" "
Balch, John Jr.†	Providence,	" "
Bicknell, Thomas W.	"	" "
Baker, William S.†	"	" "
Bradley. Charles S.	"	" "
*Brown John Carter	"	" "
Brayton, George A.†	Warwick,	" "
*Barstow, John	Providence,	" "
Barstow, Amos C. (1849)	"	" "
Barker, James T.†	"	" "
Belden, C. Dwight	"	" "
Branch. S.†	"	" "
Bishop. P. E.	Pawtucket,	" "
Barnard, Henry†	Hartford, Conn.,	" "
Bishop, Nathan.†	New York,	" "
Belden, Stanton (1849)	North Providence,	" "
Ballou, Ariel†	Woonsocket,	" "
Bennett, Charles (1860)	Westerly,	" "
Bowen, Israel M.	Johnston,	" "
Baggs, Elisha L.†	Exeter,	" "
Bates, C. G.	Coventry Centre,	" "
Belden, Francis S.	Chicago,	" "
Browning, Joseph L.	Charlestown,	" "
Bates, Benoni	Coventry,	" "
Burlingame, Ann E.	River Point,	" "
Burgess, Martha D.†	Providence,	" "
*Bowen. Esther†	"	" "
*Brown. Fenner†	"	" "
Barber, Mary F. (1860)	Westerly,	" "
Bentley, George M.	"	" "
Borden, Bailey E.	Manville,	" "
*Bosworth. Alfred†	Warren,	" "
Barber. P. M. 2d. (1860)	Ashaway,	" "
Babcock. John W. (1860)	Westerly,	" "
Babcock. Charles H. (1860)	"	" "
Babcock, Samuel A. (1860)	"	" "
Burdick. Benjamin B. (1860)	"	" "
Burdick, Mary E. (1860)	"	" "
Burlingame, Nancy M. (1860)	Woonsocket,	" "
Brown, Melissa B. (1860)	"	" "
Brown. Betsey J. (1860)	"	" "
Benson. H. A.	"	" "

15

Bushee, James	Woonsocket,	Previous to 1872.
*Boyden, Rev. John Jr.†	"	" "
Buffum, Sarah A.	"	" "
Ballou, Latimer W.†	"	" "
Ballou, George C.	"	" "
*Burgess, Thomas,†	Providence,	" "
Brown, Lucius	Fall River, Mass.,	" "
Brown, Esther E.	Summit,	" "
Benson, Marion A.	Millville,	" "
Berry, Charles P.	Chepachet,	" "
Budlong, M. E.	Cumberland,	" "
Chase, Rebecca E.	Providence,	" "
Caswell, Alexis†	"	" "
Currey, Samuel†	"	" "
Clarke, George L.†	"	" "
Clarke, Edward†	"	" "
Cooper, Larkin A.	"	" "
Carpenter, Elizabeth B.	"	" "
Clarke, Benjamin F.	"	" "
Cutler, Edward H.	"	" "
Cooke, Willis	Woonsocket,	" "
Coggeshall, S. W.	"	" "
Cooper, Varnum A.	Nashua, N. H.,	" "
Cumming, Anna	Woonsocket,	" "
Carpenter, Charles F.	Coventry,	" "
Clarke, Henry	Pawtucket,	" "
Coats, Charles	North Stonington, Conn.,	" "
Chapman, J. (1860)	Westerly,	" "
Chapin, Ruth E. (1860)	"	" "
Cottrell, Charles T. (1860)	"	" "
Clark, Elisha P. (1860)	Rockville,	" "
Chapin, Thomas B. (1860)	Westerly,	" "
Collins, A. B. (1860)	"	" "
Church, Nelson K.	Usquepaugh,	" "
Cole, George W.	Valley Falls,	" "
Cady, Isaac F.	Barrington Centre,	" "
Collins, James M.	Westerly,	" "
Cooke, N. B.	Bristol,	" "
Carpenter, Alice H.	Seekonk, Mass.,	" "
Collins, Susan E.	Phenix,	" "
*Colburn, Dana P. (1849)	Providence,	" "
Caskill, Edward B.	Woonsocket,	" "
Cragin, Frances M.	Providence,	" "
Congdon, M. Frances	"	" "
Congdon, Lydia E.	Woonsocket,	" "
Carpenter, Ellen	Cumberland,	" "
Chase, John F.	Tiverton,	" "

Cook, Rev. T. D.	Providence,	Previous to 1872.
Doyle, Sarah E.	"	" "
Dean, Sarah	"	" "
Day, Henry†	"	" "
Dixon, Nathan F.†	"	" "
Duncan, Alexander†	"	" "
DeMunn, Noble W.	"	" "
Davis, Thomas	North Providence,	" "
Darling, T. S.	Woonsocket,	" "
Davis, Franklin II. (1860)	Westerly,	" "
Davis, Oliver (1860)	"	" "
Darrow, E. R.	"	" "
*Dumont, Rev. A. H.†	Newport,	" "
*Dyer, Benjamin†	Providence,	" "
*Dwight, Gamliel L. (1849)	"	" "
Dyer, Sarah E.	Knightsville,	" "
Dyer, Maria E.	Providence,	" "
Esten, M. L.	Slatersville,	" "
Esten, Amasa Jr.	"	" "
Ewins, Margaret,	Providence,	" "
Earle, Catherine	Woonsocket,	" "
Eddy, Richard E.†	Providence,	" "
Evans, Thomas O.†	Chepachet,	" "
Edwards, James T.	East Greenwich,	" "
Edwards, Richard,	Normal School, Illinois,	" "
Esten, Rhoda A.	North Scituate,	" "
Eddy, Cornelia (1860)	Westerly,	" "
Fisher, Ellen	Woonsocket,	" "
*Field, Laura E.	Providence,	" "
Fowler, Ezekiel	Woonsocket,	" "
Farnum, Caleb†	Providence,	" "
Fry, Minerva A.	Woonsocket,	" "
Fisher, Weston A.†	Providence,	" "
Foster, A. J. (1860)	Westerly,	" ,,
Gallup, Benjamin V.	Providence,	" "
Gammell, William†	"	" "
Giddings, Joshua D.†	"	" "
Greene, Samuel S. (1849)	"	" "
Godding, Alvah W.	"	" "
Guild, Martha J.	"	" "
Greene, J. B.	"	" "
Gory, Arnold W.	Chepachet.	" "
Grover, Zwinglius†	Providence,	" "
Gray, Edward Jr.	Tiverton Four Corners,	" "
Greene, Carrie	Chepachet,	" "
Greene, Eliza C.	"	" "
Gorton, Jason W.	Summit,	" "

Greene, Samuel	Woonsocket,	Previous to 1872.
Greene. Susan M.	Bristol,	" "
Gorton, Hannah H.	Warwick,	" "
Greene, John T.	Coventry,	" "
Gruber, Frances	Providence,	" "
Greenman, B. F.	Charlestown,	" "
Gorton, Abbie A.	Escoheag,	" "
Gallup, Sarah B.	Collamer, Conn.,	" "
Guy, Helen F.	Davisville,	" "
*Gamwell, Albert A.†	Providence,	" "
*Greene, Phebe A.	"	" "
*Hutchins, Shubael†	"	" "
Howard, E. H.	"	" "
Harkness, Albert†	"	" "
Haskell, Ellen M.	"	" "
Helme, Harriet J.	"	" "
Haskell, Ruth A.	"	" "
Hoyt, David W.	"	" "
Haile, Levi	Warren,	" "
Hendrick, C. A.	Woonsocket,	" "
Hendrick, Fanny	"	" "
*Harris, Edward	"	" "
Harkness, Hiram	Smithfield,	" "
Harkness, James T.	"	" "
Hull, Harriet K.	Kingston,	" "
Hazard, Thomas P.†	"	" "
Hall, Charles H. (1860)	Westerly,	" "
Hazard, Harriet C. (1860)	"	" "
Hoxie, George W. (1860)	Shannock Mills.	" "
Hinkley, Charles H. (1860)	Westerly,	" "
Hutchins, Charles	Providence,	" "
Hammett, John L.	"	" "
Hopkins. Rev. George O.	North Scituate,	" "
Hoag, Emily	Lonsdale,	" "
Hicks, Charles R.	Fall River, Mass.,	" "
Hill, Byron R.	Cranston,	" "
Holt, Emma F.	Blackstone, Mass.,	" "
Howard, Henry	Phenix,	" "
Harvey, Resolved	Coventry,	" "
Hoag, Caroline D.	Woonsocket,	" "
Holmes, Harvey *	Bristol,	" "
Holmes, Mary E.	North Stonington, Conn.,	" "
Holdredge, Geo. W. (1849)		" "
Haines. T. V.	Crompton,	" "
Ives, Robert H.†	Providence,	" "
*Ives, Moses B.†	"	" "
Ingalls, Elkanah	Cranston,	" "

Jencks, Mary T.	Pawtucket,	Previous to 1872.
Jennings, John	Woonsocket,	" "
Kingsbury, John†	Providence,	" "
Keith, Christopher T.†	"	" "
King, Mary	"	" "
Kent, William S.	North Scituate,	" "
Kent, John R.	Phenix.	" "
Kenyon, Peleg	Hopkinton,	" "
Keith, William S.	River Point,	" "
Kendall, Joshua	Bristol,	" "
Kenyon, Henry B.	Alton,	" "
Knapp, Mary A.	Chepachet,	" "
Kimball, D. W.	Woonsocket,	" "
Keach, Clovis E.	Burrillville,	" "
*Kile. O. H.	Westerly,	" "
Knowles, Horatio N. Jr.	Wakefield,	" "
King, E. A.	Pascoag,	" "
*Lawton, Edward W.†	Newport,	" "
Leach, Rev. Daniel (1856)	Providence,	" "
Lyon, Merrick†	"	" "
Lyon, Emory,	"	" "
Latham, Cornelia W.	"	" "
Lewis. Celia J.	"	" "
*Lockwood, Moses B.†	"	" "
Larkin, R. S. (1860)	Westerly,	" "
Lewis, Mary C.	Providence.	" "
Lewis, Nathan B.	Exeter,	" "
Lincoln, A. J.	Coventry,	" "
Ladd, John J. (1860)	Providence,	" "
LeCard, George	Coventry,	" "
Matteson, Benjamin W.	"	" "
Mowry, William A. (1859)	Providence,	" "
Metcalf, Edwin†	"	" "
*Mason. Owen†	"	" "
May, Amasa	"	" "
Miles. Amanda	"	" "
Mowry, Jenks A.†	"	" "
Metcalf. William	Woonsocket,	" "
Morley, Frank G.	Bristol,	" "
Munroe, Abby D.	"	" "
Matteson. Braman W.	Coventry,	" "
Maxon, Abby M. (1860)	Westerly,	" "
Maxon, Charlotte A. (1860)	"	" "
Maxon. Charles A. (1860)	"	" "
Mann, Rev. Joel	Kingston,	" "
Manchester, George†	South Portsmouth,	" "
Morse, Guilford	Springfield, Mass.,	" "

Name	Location	Previous to 1872
Magill, Edward H.	Providence,	Previous to 1872.
Mason, Ambrose B.	Warren,	" "
Monroe, Clara E.	Manville,	" "
Macomber, Joseph E	Portsmouth,	" "
*Meggette, M. M.	Woonsocket.	" "
Meader, A. A.	Cumberland,	" "
Miller, Maria F. (1860)	Allenton,	" "
Miner, G. H. (1860)	Westerly.	" "
*Nash, H. C.	Portland, Me.,	" "
Newell, George E.	Pawtucket,	" "
Niles, Julia A.,	Woonsocket,	" "
Nichols, Celia A.	Greene,	" "
Nichols, Helen A.	Providence,	" "
Newbury, Sarah (1860)	Westerly,	" "
Osborn, Sarah	Woonsocket,	" "
Osborn, Esther	"	" "
Osgood, Rev Samuel†	Providence,	" "
Osgood, J. Anna	"	" "
Olney, John†	"	" "
Pitman, Joseph S.†	"	" "
Perry, Amos†	"	" "
*Patten, William S.†	"	" "
Purkis, Sarah A.	"	" "
Phelon. Rev. Benjamin	"	" "
Padelford, Adelaide D.	"	" "
Perrin, Mrs. Daniel	"	" "
Potter, Hon. Elisha R.†	South Kingstown,	" "
Parker, James E.	Johnston,	" "
*Peck, Allen O.†	Providence,	" "
Pendleton, Anne L. (1860)	Westerly,	" "
Pendleton, Kate (1860)	"	" "
Pendleton, Sarah E (1860)	"	" "
Perrin, Alice (1860)	"	" "
Potter, J. B.	Greene,	" "
Phillips, S.	Georgiaville,	" "
Peckham Anginette (1860)	Westerly,	" "
Palmer, Hannah (1860)	Stonington, Conn.,	" "
Prosser, P. S.	Carolina Mills,	" "
Page, Maria W.	Pascoag,	" "
Page, Susan A.	"	" "
Payne, Nancy A.	"	" "
Place, H. Lester	Mt. Vernon, R. I.,	" "
Potter, S. A.	Providence,	" "
Potter, Thomas G.	East Providence,	" "
Paine, Minerva J.	Slatersville,	" "
Pickett, Horace W.	Tiverton,	" "
Porter, Aaron	Bristol,	" "

Park, Mary F.	Woonsocket,	Previous to 1872.
Paine, Julia A.	"	" "
Paine, Cordelia E.	"	" "
Pitts, Susie A.	"	" "
Paine, S. Madeline	North Blackstone,	" "
Paine, Minnie J.	Slatersville,	" "
Quereau, G W.	East Greenwich,	" "
Robinson, J. H. (1860)	Westerly,	" "
Reynolds, Benjamin (1860)	"	" "
Rich, Ezekiel	Bristol,	" "
Reynolds, Russell W.	Richmond,	" "
Ralph, Betsey T.	Fisherville,	" "
Rodman, Samuel†	Providence,	" "
Rathbun, Mary E.	"	" "
Russell, Levi W.	"	" "
Remington, Frances A.	"	" "
Robbins, Alvin C.	Millville ss ,	" "
Ray, Joel R.	Providence,	" "
Stone, Rev. Edwin M. (1848)	"	" "
Stockwell, Thomas B.	"	" "
Steere, Mattie C.	"	" "
Smith, James Y.	"	" "
Smith, Lewis B.	"	" "
Seagraves, Joseph	"	" "
Steoent, Phebe A.†	"	" "
Scammell, S. S.	"	" "
Stanton, Kate S.	"	" "
Stivers, John H.	"	" "
Spencer, H. L.	"	" "
Sheldon, Jeremiah†	"	" "
Sawin, James M.	"	" "
Stebbins, Fannie	"	" "
Stockbridge, Rev. J. C.	"	" "
Sheldon, William†	"	" "
Stillman, Mary A (1860)	Westerly.	" "
Stillman, Harriet W. (1860)	"	" "
Stillman, James (1860)	"	" "
Saunders, T. C. (1860)	Potter's Hill,	" "
Sayles, William R.	Cumberland Hill,	" "
Seamans, Layton E.	Coventry,	" "
Sisson, Asa	Anthony,	" "
Seagrave, A. R.	Uxbridge, Mass.,	" "
Staples, Thomas B.	Slatersville,	" "
Shumway, Annie M.	Pascoag,	" "
Stanfield, B. B.	"	" "
Slade, Georgianna A.	"	" "

Shumway, Mary E.	Pascoag,	Previous to 1872.
Smith, Eliza	Providence,	" "
Spencer, H. L.	Anthony,	" "
Steere, Diana J.	Woonsocket,	" "
Steere. Joanna A.	"	" "
Steere, William A.	"	" "
Spencer, D. P.	Peace Dale,	" "
Sheffield, William P.†	Newport,	" "
Stone, Harriet A. (1860)	Stonington, Conn..	" "
Stanton, Charles	North Stonington, Conn..	" "
Stone. Hiram	Foster,	" "
Slocum, Mrs. Z. O.	Chepachet,	" "
Steere, Laura M.	Manton,	" "
Steere, Fannie M.	"	" "
Shaw, Jedediah	Little Compton,	" "
*Stone, James L. (1849)	Providence,	" "
Sisson, Joseph T.†	North Providence,	" "
Slater, Horatio N.†	Providence,	" "
Stone, Dexter S.	Philadelphia, Pa.,	" "
Seamans, Ira O.	Phenix,	" "
Shaw, Emma	Thompson, Conn.,	" "
Shaw, Mary C.	Centreville.	" "
Shepard, Rev. Thomas†	Bristol,	" "
Stimson, John J.	Providence,	" "
Sheffield, Hannah (1860)	Westerly.	" "
Sayles, Henry C.	Woonsocket.	" "
Scott, Livingston	"	" "
Salisbury, Phebe A.	Lime Rock,	" "
Spencer, Lydia C.	Warwick,	" "
Talcott, James M.	Providence,	" "
Tingley, L. Sophia	"	" "
Tourtellot, Jesse S.†	Glocester,	" "
*Tillinghast, George S.	Foster,	" "
*Tillinghast, George H.†	Providence.	" "
Tillinghast, Joseph	Summit,	" "
Tallman, John B †	Woonsocket,	" "
Thurber. Samuel	Providence,	" "
Thayer, Lucy A.	New Boston, Conn..	" "
Thompson, Phebe H. (1860)	Westerly,	" "
Thompson, Benjamin F. (1860)	"	" "
Taylor, John A. (1860)	"	" "
Tillinghast, E. A.	Coventry,	" "
Tefft, J. H.	Kingston,	" "
Tolman, W. E.	Pawtucket,	" "
Tyler, Susan A.†	Providence,	" "
*Tobey, Samuel B.†	"	" "
Taft, Mary E.	Blackstone,	" "

Taft, B. P.	Burrillville,	Previous to 1872.
*Updike, Wilkins†	Providence.	" "
Vincent, Thomas	Westerly.	" "
Vernon, Thomas†	Providence,	" "
Verry, Perley	Woonsocket.	" "
Varney, George F.	Sandwich, N. H.	" "
Vose, E. F. (1860)	Westerly,	" "
Wardwell, George T.	Woonsocket,	" "
*Wayland, Rev. Francis†	Providence.	" "
Woods, Rev. Alva	"	" "
Webb, Rev. Samuel H.	"	" "
Waterman, Emily F.	"	" "
Westcott, S. Lizzie	"	" "
Whipple, Amasa C.	Attleboro. Mass.,	" "
Whittemore, Gilbert E.	Providence,	" "
Wood, Henry A.	East Greenwich	" "
Williams, H. W.	Foster,	" "
Williams, Albert S.	North Foster,	" "
Winsor, Nancy W.	Greenville,	" "
Wheelock, Lucius A. (1849)	Providence,	" "
Wilson, George C.	Manville,	" "
Waldron, W. H.	Pascoag.	" "
Walden, Elizabeth F.	Chepachet,	" "
Wade, Mrs. James	Pascoag.	" "
White, Abbie M.	Burrillville,	" "
Wood, Allen F.	River Point,	" "
Wynn. Mary	Pascoag,	" "
Woodbridge, Wm. H. Jr. (1860)	Westerly,	" "
*Young, Edward R.†	Providence,	" "
Young. L. R.†	"	" "

Allen, Stella C.	Providence,	January 1872.
Alden, Sarah C.	"	" "
Angell, Sarah C	"	" "
Arnold, Dr. S. Augustus	"	" "
Allen, Juliet A.	"	" "
Allen, Mrs. Henry	"	" "
Adams, Mary C. B.	"	" "
Armington, Hattie A.	Pawtuxet,	" "
Arnold, Gertrude E.	Woonsocket,	" "
Adams, Annie J.	Pawtucket,	" "
Austin, Emily C.	Summit,	" "
*Alvord, Caleb M.	East Greenwich.	" "
Allen, Jane H.	Cranston,	" "
Allen, Hattie A.	Blackstone, Mass.,	" "
Arnold, Elveton Jr.,	North Kingstown.	" "

17

Avery, Miss A E.	Providence,	January, 1873.
Anthony, Mary E.	"	" "
Andrews, Miss E. E.	"	" "
Anthony, Susan E.	"	" "
Armstrong, Lydia	"	" "
Allen, Daniel G.	North Kingstown,	" "
Albro, Christopher D.	Portsmouth,	" "
Almy, Margaret G.	Newport,	" "
Arnold, Francis E.	Jamestown,	" "
Anthony, Albert L.	Swansey, Mass.,	" "
Bacon, Sarah J.	Providence,	January, 1872.
Beane, Elsie A.	"	" "
Bartlett, Mary E.	"	" "
Brown, Allen	"	" "
Bolster, Jerome B.	"	" "
Bell, George	"	" "
Bucklin, R. Anna C.	"	" " ,
Babcock, M. Austania	"	" "
Bancroft, Susan C.	"	" "
Bartlett, Addie A.	"	" "
Brown, Ella A.	Spragueville,	" "
Babcock, Jennie H.	Westerly,	" "
Buffington, Geraldine	Warren,	" "
Babcock, S. A.	North Stonington, Conn.,	" "
Briggs, Stephen A.	Stonington Conn.,	" "
Bodfish, Joshua L.	East Greenwich,	" "
Baker, Sarah	"	" "
Ballou, Desire F.	Lonsdale,	" "
Bates, Benoni	Coventry,	" "
Brown, Arthur W.	Middletown,	" "
Bowen, Susan K.	Summit,	" "
Burlingame, William C.	Cumberland Hill,	" "
Brown, Annie S.	Pawtuxet,	" "
Bosworth, Rebecca T.	Newport,	" "
Boss, Lizzie C.	"	" "
Brown, Lizzie	Pawtucket,	" "
Bates. C. G.	Coventry Centre,	" "
Barker, Mrs. C. J.	Tiverton,	" "
Bucklyn, John K.	Mystic Bridge, Conn.,	" "
Bates, John A.	West Greenwich Centre,	" "
Ballou, Amanda J.	Georgiaville,	" "
Brown, Ella M.	Harmony,	" "
Bowen, J. A.	Boston,	" "
Bowen, L. A.	East Greenwich,	" "
Brown, Ann E.	Tiverton,	" "
Bowen, Fanny W.	South Attleboro',	" "
Brown, Ellen M.	Providence,	January, 1873.

Name	Place	Date
Behan Ann M.	Providence,	January, 1873.
Belden, C. Dwight	"	" "
Bellows, L. M.	North Providence,	" "
Brown, Isadore	"	" "
Barker, C. W.	Tiverton,	" "
Bates, Nellie	West Greenwich Centre,	" "
Bartlett, Addie M.	Mapleville,	" "
Bryant, S. Fannie	Woonsocket,	" "
Bryant, Addie G.	Medway Village, Mass.,	" "
Bates, Hattie N.	Pascoag,	" "
Bowen, Helen M.	Chepachet,	" "
Barnes, Irene C.	Greenville,	" "
Bailey, Thomas T.	Boston,	" "
Barber, Lizzie	Westerly,	January, 1874.
Burlingame, N. M.	Woonsocket,	" "
Barrows, Sarah	Pawtucket,	" "
Barber, A. E.	Woonsocket,	" "
Brown, M. A.		" "
Bowen, Hannah		" "
Brown, Sarah W. A.	Middletown,	" "
Barrows, L. A.		" "
Blakeslee, T. D.	East Greenwich,	" "
Carpenter, Elizabeth B.	Providence,	January, 1872.
Cooke, Emma E.	"	" "
Carrigan, Helen A.	"	" "
Case, Mattie	"	" "
Cross, F. E.	"	" "
Chase, Elizabeth J.	"	" "
Chase, William E.	Kingston,	" "
Gardner, Edwin R.	Providence,	" "
Chillson, Henry	"	" "
Church, Mary E.	Charlestown,	" "
Chappell, Sarah J.	Wakefield,	" "
Cook, Helen M.	Providence,	" "
Cunliff, Eliza P.	"	" "
Coggeshall, Belle J.	Bristol,	" "
Cornell, Imogene R.	Apponaug,	" "
Collins, Amy F.	North Providence,	" "
Chase, Anna P.	Manville,	" "
Clarke, Minnie L.	Albion,	" "
Clark, Henry	Pawtucket,	" "
Collins, Francis W.	Narragansett Pier,	" "
Chase, Anna G.	Newport,	" "
Chase, Emily B.	"	" "
Carpenter, Belle F.	Cumberland Hill,	" "
Clarke, Rebecca C.	Albion,	" "
Clarke, B. F.	Newport,	" "

Clarke, J. P.	Exeter,	January, 1872.
Crandall, Stephen G.	Adamsville,	" "
Chappell, M. Hortense	Carolina,	" "
Cole, Martha D.	Warren,	" "
Case, James G.	East Providence,	" "
Clarke, Thomas H.	Newport,	" "
Clarke, Henry W.	"	" "
Clarke, George	Wyoming.	" "
Cooke, H. E.	Slatersville,	" "
Church, George S.	Providence,	January, 1873.
Carpenter, E. J.	"	" "
Conant, Rev. W. H.	"	" "
Chace, Harriet R.	"	" "
Chapin, Mary E.	"	" "
Cobb, D. A.	"	" "
Cutting, Phebe A.	"	" "
Conley, Mary L.	"	" "
Carpenter, Miss L. M.	"	" "
Coe, Marcy	"	" "
Cole, Mary M.	Clayville,	" "
Cargill, Malvina	Valley Falls,	" "
Carpenter, George E.	Watchemoket,	" "
Cooke, John T.	South Portsmouth,	" "
Clarke, Hannah E.	Wakefield,	" "
Carr, J. P.	Jamestown,	" "
Collins, Peleg	Anthony,	" "
Church, Calista	Tiverton.	" "
Comstock, Amy L.	Burrillville,	January, 1874.
Chase, Charles A.	Woonsocket,	" "
Chase, Rev. B. A.	Diamond Hill,	" "
Chesbro, Mrs. A. L.	Providence,	" "
Chase, Mr. W. E.		" "
Chase, Charles A.		" "
Collins, Nancy	Providence,	" "
Collins, Lizzie E.	"	" "
Chase, H. J.	Newport,	" "
Dawley, Edward	Bristol,	January, 1872.
Davis, Hattie	Davisville,	" "
DeWolf, Lizzie P.	Wakefield,	" "
Dixon, Irene	Rocky Brook,	" "
Denaly, Kate	Providence,	" "
Doran, Belle	Pawtucket,	" "
Darling, Katie	Millville, Mass.,	" "
Durfee, Joshua T.	Fall River, Mass.,	" "
Daggett, M. Isabel	Providence,	January, 1873.
Donnavan, Joanna	"	" "
Davis, Mrs. Thomas	Pawtucket.	January, 1874.

Eastman, J.	East Greenwich,	January, 1872.
Ela, Rev. David H.	"	" "
Esten, Ida L.	Pawtucket,	January, 1873.
Ewins, Margaret	Providence,	January, 1874.
Faxon, Charles E.	"	January, 1872.
Field, Laura E.	"	" "
Freeman, Lester A.	"	" "
Fry, Mary E.	Carolina Mills,	" "
Fairman, Mary C.	Pawtucket,	" "
Fitz, Frank	"	" "
Friend, R. M.	Newport,	" "
Fry, Mattie	Carolina Mills,	" "
Fuller, Rev. O. P.	Centreville,	" "
Fielden, Mrs. Annie F.	Providence,	January, 1873.
Fales, Sarah E.	Newport,	" "
Frethingham, Mary A.	"	" "
Fisher, Annie	Olneyville,	" "
Gould, Edwin W.	Providence,	January, 1872.
Gladding, Lucy J.	"	" "
Griswold, Mrs. E. A.	"	" "
Greenough, J. C.	"	" "
Gates, Charles H.	"	" "
Gushee, L. L.	Warren,	" "
Gordon, Mary L.	Pawtucket,	" "
Gardiner, Mrs. Bessie	Usquepangh,	" "
Greene, Martha A.	Slocumville,	" "
Gray, Peace C.	Tiverton Four Corners,	" "
Gifford, Miss L. A.	Adamsville,	" "
Grinnell, H. B. M. Mrs.	Pawtuxet,	" "
Gardiner, Henry G.	"	" "
Gorton, Miss H. F.	Newport,	" "
Gorton, Miss Etta C.	"	" "
Greene, Alice M.	Pawtucket,	" "
Greene, A. E. Miss	Newport,	" "
Gardner, Ida M.	Laurel Hill,	" "
Grant, Orville B.	Providence,	January, 1873.
Greene, Millen S.	Carolina Mills,	" "
Greene, Albert	Westerly,	January, 1874.
Greene, Ann E.	Newport,	" "
Harvey, Clara B.	Providence,	January, 1872.
Hazard, Rosa E. G.	"	" "
Hyde, Fred A.	"	" "
Hussey, Emma P.	"	" "
Hall, J. Milton	"	" "
Hewitt, Harriet E.	"	" "
Heywood, Almira L.	"	" "
Harris, Louise O.	"	" "

Kenneth, John	Wyoming,	January, 1872.
Keach. J. A.	Centredale,	" "
Keith, Stillman H.	South Manchester, Conn.,	" "
King. Mrs. Celia A.	Providence,	January, 1873.
Kelton, Fannie	"	" "
King, Edwin H.	Watchemoket,	" "
Kenyon, Henry	Wyoming,	" "
Kenyon, D C.	East Greenwich,	" "
Keyser, R. S.	"	January, 1874.
Leavens, Rosamond R.	Providence,	January, 1872.
Leavitt. Miss C. E.	"	" "
Lyon, Abbie F.	Centreville,	" "
Lincoln, M.	Coventry,	" "
Lawton, Eliza H.	Tiverton,	" "
Lawton, Mrs. E. T.	"	" "
Lillibridge, Sarah M.	Richmond,	" "
Lawton. A. A.	Voluntown,	" "
Lillibridge, A. A.	Wyoming,	" "
Locke, Hannah W.	Usquepaugh,	" "
Lewis, Martha B.	Exeter,	" "
Littlefield, N. W.	Newport,	" "
Lathrop, M. E.	"	" "
Lincoln. Susan	Providence,	December, 1872.
Lincoln, Eugene H.	"	" "
LeFavor, H.	Central Falls,	January, 1873.
Lyon, Fannie M.	Centreville,	" "
LeFavor. Julia		" "
Murray, M. Addie	Providence,	January, 1872.
Magill, Edward H.	"	" "
Manchester, A. J.	"	" "
Mann. Carrie	"	" "
Martin. Jennie	Warren,	" "
Mowry, J. E.	North Providence,	" "
Marble, Sarah	Woonsocket,	" "
Monroe, William C.	"	" "
Moore, H. B.	Exeter,	" "
Meader, L. H.	Albion,	" "
Moore, Andrew B.	Usquepaugh,	" "
Moore. L. E.	"	" "
Moore. M. A.	"	" "
Morey, Philip A.	"	" "
Miller, Ella A.	Barrington Centre,	" "
Maryott. C. A.	North Stonington, Conn.,	" "
Miller, Belle	Manton,	" "
Maxon, Abbie M.	Westerly,	" "
Martin. M. S.	Newport,	" "
Miner, H. E	North Stonington, Conn.,	" "

Name	Place	Date
Mills, James C.	Pawtucket,	January, 1872.
Maryatt. C. E.	North Stonington, Conn.,	" "
Morse, Nancy E.	Woonsocket,	" "
Manchester, Clara	Olneyville,	December, 1872.
Morgan, Mrs. Vana L.	Providence.	January, 1873.
Macdonald, Julia E.	"	" "
Magoon, B. S.	"	" "
Metcalf, Abbie B.	"	" "
Maxfield, L. G.	"	" "
Merriam, W. W.	Exeter,	" "
Magoon, Mrs. Benjamin	Olneyville,	" "
Mowry, S. Nellie	Georgiaville,	" "
Magoon, Mrs. J. R.	Centreville,	" "
Martin, W. E.	Natick,	" "
Mowry, Eliza A.	Providence,	January, 1874.
Mowry, Viola J.	"	" "
Nettleton, F. H.	Clinton,	January, 1872
Newton, J. T.	Pendleton Hill,	" "
Nichols, Miss O. E.	Providence,	" "
Neville, C. A.	North Providence,	" "
Northup. Mary E,	Centreville,	" "
Northup, Sarah C.	Providence,	January, 1873.
Nye. J. M	Centreville,	" "
Oldfield, Mary H.	Providence,	January, 1872.
Owen. Lizzie	"	" "
Padelford, Gov. Seth	"	" "
Peck, Annie S	"	" "
Peck, George B.	"	" "
Packard, C. M.	"	" "
Perry, Emma	Pawtucket.	" "
Potter, Minnie P.	Central Falls,	" "
Pitman, Julia F.	Newport,	" "
Pitcher, Fannie I.	East Greenwich,	" "
Pratt Lizzie F.	Lonsdale,	" "
Paine, E. Lizzie	Pawtucket,	" "
Parker, Ezra K.	Coventry,	" "
Paige. Nellie E.	Slatersville,	" "
Peck, William T.	Warren,	" "
Peabody, Miss J. S.	Newport,	" "
Phillips, Mowry	Pascoag,	" "
Potter, Lydia H.	"	" "
Phillips, William H.	Olneyville,	December, 1872.
Perry, William H.	Charlestown,	" "
Potter, Carrie C.	Providence,	January, 1873
Perry, Mrs. Sarah M. H.	Uxbridge, Mass.,	" "
Prosser, Mary J.	Wakefield,	" "
Peckham, Alice	Westerly,	" "

Name	Place	Date
Phillips, Lilla	Pascoag,	January, 1873.
Paterson, Ernestine	North Foster,	" "
Palsey, Abbie J.	Rockland,	" "
Potter, Abbie	East Greenwich,	" "
Paine, Lizzie M.	Central Falls,	" "
Paine, Melvina	"	" "
Park, Mary F.	Woonsocket,	January, 1874.
Robinson, Lizzie S.	Providence,	January, 1872.
Reynolds, Myrtie	"	" "
Robinson, Joseph K.	"	" "
Rickard, William W.	"	" "
Read, Miss G. D.	"	" "
Reynolds, Mary B.	North Kingstown,	" "
Rea, Hattie L.	Barrington,	" "
Ray, Adeline	Exeter,	" "
Reynolds, T. O.	Chepachet,	" "
Reynolds, Mary E.	North Kingstown,	" "
Reynolds, Amanda E.	Chepachet,	" "
Rhoades, Benjamin H.	Newport,	" "
Ray, Sarah M.	Watchemoket,	January, 1873.
Richards, J. S.	Cranston,	" "
Rounds, Cynthia	South Foster,	" "
Russell, Maria J.	Pawtuxet,	" "
Riley, Mary A.	Westerly,	" "
Salisbury, Adela C.	Providence,	January, 1872.
Swan, Allen L.	"	" "
Salisbury, Ellen A.	"	" "
Swift, Clara L.	"	" "
Shepley, Mary B.	"	" "
Sayles, Emeline A.	"	" "
Scott, Annie E.	"	" "
Searle, Miss A. E.	"	" "
Salmon, Mary	"	" "
Stetson, Mary S.	"	" "
Shaw, Emma	"	" "
Salisbury, Susan	"	December, 1872.
Snow, Sophie P.	Phenix,	January, 1872.
Sherman, Lizzie C.	Valley Falls,	" "
Sisson, Alice M.	Anthony,	" "
Stillman, Hattie E.	Westerly,	" "
Smith, Eliza B.	"	" "
Stillman, George C.	North Stonington, Conn.,	" "
Sherman, Charles H.	Exeter,	" "
Sheldon, Lizzie C.	Wakefield,	" "
Swinburne, Elizabeth H.	Newport,	" "
Salisbury, Emma F.	South Scituate,	" "
Sutton, Emma F.	Watchemoket,	" "

18

Simmons, Hattie B.	Pawtucket,	January, 1872.
Simmons, A. R.	Lonsdale,	" "
Smith, Mary C.	Pawtuxet,	" "
Snow, S. A.	Uxbridge, Mass.,	" "
Steere, Isaac	Burrillville.	" "
Small, A. D.	Newport,	" "
Scarborough, Mary E.	Providence,	January, 1873.
Swan, Harriet A.	"	" "
Stephens, Abbie F.	"	" "
Stanley, Lucy C.	"	" "
Sheffield, Mary C.	"	" "
Snow, Etta	"	" "
Sweet, S. S.	"	" "
Simmons, J. W.	Franklin, N. H.,	" "
Sayles, H. C.	Bristol,	" "
Smart, Charles H.	Woonsocket.	" "
Spencer, Deacon Orin	Coventry.	" "
Shove, Miss M. A.	Westerly.	" "
Sherman, Lilian M.	Burrillville,	January, 1874.
Steere, Mrs. Emeline E.	"	" "
Stanley, Miss L. C.		" "
Snell, Helen L.	Providence,	" "
Steere, Ida E.		" "
Smith, A. A.	Providence,	" "
Steele, Charlotte E.	Pawtucket,	" "
Saunders, A. A., M. D.		" "
Tillinghast, C. E.	Griswold, Conn.,	January, 1872.
Tefft, Edward C.	Kingston,	" "
Tefft, Ann E.	"	" "
Tillinghast, Leonard A.	Greene.	" "
Thornton, Ella M.	Providence,	" "
Terry, Mary E.	"	" "
Taylor, B. P.	"	" "
Tiffany, R. A.	Barrington.	" "
Tillinghast, Ira L.	Wyoming,	" "
Tiffany, Miss E. R.	Barrington,	" "
Tucker, William F.	Shannock Mills,	" "
Tompkins, Eleanor L.	Adamsville,	" "
Thurber, Martha F.	Providence,	January, 1873.
Taft, Maria L.	"	" "
Tinkler, Rosa	"	" "
Tillinghast, Iva L.	Wyoming,	" "
Tanner, Abel	Carolina Mills,	January, 1874.
Tefft, Azel W.		" "
Vincent. Charles G.	Rockville,	January, 1872.
Vestal, Tilghman R.	Columbia, Tenn.,	" "
Vose. P. C.	Woonsocket,	" "

Watson, Carrie	Kingston,	January, 1872.
Waldron, Sarah A.	Wakefield,	" "
Willoughby, Lilian R.	Providence,	" "
Wood, Mary E.	"	" "
, Williams, Alonzo	"	" "
Whittemore, Julia B.	"	" "
White, Hattie	Woonsocket,	" "
Williams, Amy M.	Crompton,	" "
Wood, Caroline A.	Watchemoket,	" "
Wood, M. Lizzie	Newport,	" "
Walker, W. S.	Olneyville,	" "
Williams, S. Lila	North Providence,	" "
Walker, Flora L.	"	" "
Willard, M. H.	Warwick Neck,	" "
Woodward, Ada	East Providence,	" "
Whaley, Mary A.	Newport,	" "
Whipple, Emily F.	Coventry,	" "
Wood, Sarah E.	Watchemoket,	" "
Winsor, Ella J.	Greenville,	" "
Woodart, E. M.	Woonsocket,	" "
Whipple, Mary C.	Olneyville,	" "
Wing, F. W.	North Providence,	" "
Warner, Prof. W. W.	Providence,	January, 1873.
Willis, Mrs. Edwin	"	" "
White, Mrs. Rebecca H.	"	" "
Wallace, Nellie	"	" "
Watson, Rev. E. F.	Wakefield,	" "
Wood, Ellen P.	Greene,	" "
Waterman, W. W.	Taunton,	" "
Wentworth, Miss M. C.	Westerly,	" "
Wellman, Mrs. Almira R.	Chepachet,	" "
Wilcox, Abbie E.	Niantic,	January, 1874.
Woodward, Emily		" "

CORRECTION.—In the preceding list of members John J. Stinson should have been marked with an asterisk (*) and a †; John Carter Brown with a †; and Rev. Alva Woods, D. D., with a †.

Hon. JOHN KINGSBURY.—Note, pp. 28, 42, 96.

As the last sheet of this volume was passing through the press, the sad announcement of Mr. Kingsbury's death was made. He died at his residence, on Angell street, Providence, December 21, 1874. aged 73 years. The following notice of the deceased is copied, with a few changes, from the *Providence Daily Journal* of December 22d.

Mr. KINGSBURY was a native of South Coventry, Connecticut, and was born in May, 1801. He was educated at Brown University, where he graduated with distinguished rank as a scholar in the class of 1826. While yet a student, within a few weeks of his graduation, having already fixed upon teaching as his chosen profession, he became associated with the late Mr. G. A. Dewitt, in the instruction and management of the Providence High School, at that time the principal school in the city. At the end of two years he commenced the "Young Ladies' High School," at the solicitation of many leading citizens of Providence, who had long felt the need of such an establishment for the education of their daughters. The new school, both in its instruction and in all its appointments, was of a higher grade than had been before known in this community. In 1818, he erected on Benefit street, from plans drawn by the late Thomas A. Tefft, the fine school building now occupied by Rev. J. C. Stockbridge, D. D. This school he maintained with unexampled prosperity for thirty years, during which he superintended the education of two generations of a large proportion of the foremost women of Providence, and of many from abroad. He retired from his long and most successful work in 1858, and the occasion was celebrated by a reunion of all who had been his pupils who were still among the living, with testimonials of gratitude and respect, most honorable alike to the pupils and to their veteran instructor and friend. He had already received the appointment of State Commissioner of Public Schools, which had been offered him by the Governor, so soon as his purpose was known of retiring from the labors of his school. This position he resigned in 1859, and was immediately made President of the Washington Insurance Company, an office which he continued to hold to the time of his death.

Though the founder and instructor of a private school, on which he depended for his living, he was, from the beginning, one of the most earnest and active friends and promoters of public education. and that too, long before any system for this purpose had been established in Rhode Island, and when the advocacy of such a system was anything but a passport to popularity. He did as much as any one in bringing public opinion to sanction and demand the legislation by which our present common schools were created, and he gave a vast amount of time and effort to the encouragement and guidance of those who superintended their early struggles for existence. He was the most active founder and long the President of the "Rhode Island Institute of Instruction," which did so much to sustain the labors of Mr. Barnard, the first Commissioner of our State schools, and in a great variety of ways he rendered services which, possibly, no other man among us at that time would have been able to render. In promotion of the general cause of education he also assisted in founding the "American Institute of Instruction," that national association of teachers, which has contributed so largely to the elevation of the teachers' profession throughout the country. He was the President of this body for two years, and for more than twenty years one of its councillors and managers.

In the early scientific pursuits of the "Franklin Society," Mr. KINGS-BURY took a leading part, and was for several years President of the Society. He has been for the past twenty years one of the trustees of the "Butler Hospital for the Insane," and has given much attention to the interests of that institution. In 1844 he was chosen a member of the Board of Trustees of Brown University, and in this capacity he has rendered most useful services to the place of his education. He has ever since been actively engaged not only in its immediate management, but also in the efforts which from time to time have been set on foot for increasing its endowments and enlarging its usefulness. In 1853 he was raised to its Board of Fellows, and at the same time was chosen Secretary of the Corporation, an office which he continued to hold to the end of his life. In recognition of his various and eminent services to the cause of education, the University, in 1856, conferred on him the honorary degree of Doctor of Laws.

On coming to Providence, as a student in the college, in 1822, Mr. KINGSBURY connected himself with the Richmond Street Congregational Church, and of the interests of that church he was long a most efficient promoter. When in 1851 it was proposed by a portion of its members to establish the Central Congregational Church, and to erect a new house of worship, in another part of the city, he was by common consent placed at the head of the movement. In connection with both of these churches he has through life been eminent as a teacher of the Bible. The Sunday class which he early established, and maintained, we believe, nearly to the end of his life, has embraced not only large numbers of young men of the city, but first and last, upwards of two hundred students of the University. He was for many years at the head of the Young Men's Bible Society, and also for several years, President of the Young Men's Christian Association

It is services such as these, generously and quietly rendered to so many of the most important educational, social and religious interests of the community, that have ennobled the career which we have thus imperfectly sketched.

STATE COMMISSIONERS.

NAMES.					Years. served.
Henry Barnard,	·	·	·	·	1845 to 1849. 4 years.
Elisha R. Potter, Jr.,					1849 to 1851. 5 "
Robert Allyn, ·	·	·	·	·	1854 to 1857. 3 "
John Kingsbury,		·	·	·	1857 to 1859. 2 "
Joshua B. Chapin,	·	·	·	·	1859 to 1861. 2 "
" "				·	1863 to 1863. 6 "
Henry Rousmaniere,					1861 to 1863. 2 "
Thomas W. Bicknell,	·	·	·	·	1869 to 1875. 6 "
Thomas B. Stockwell, ·	·	·	·	·	1875 to

SUPERINTENDENTS OF SCHOOLS.—1874-75.*

TOWN OR CITY.	SUPERINTENDENT.	POST OFFICE ADDRESS.
Providence, ·	Rev. Daniel Leach, · ·	Providence.
Newport. · ·	Thomas H. Clarke, · · · ·	Newport.
Barrington.	Isaac F. Cady, A. M., · ·	Barrington Centre.
Bristol, · ·	Robert S. Andrews, ·	Bristol.
Burrillville,	Rev. William Fitz,	Pascoag.
Charlestown, ·	William F. Tucker, ·	Shannock Mills.
Coventry, ·	E. K. Parker, · ·	Summit.
Cranston,		
Cumberland,	Francis S. Weeks, · ·	Woonsocket.
East Greenwich,	Peleg G. Kenyon, · ·	East Greenwich.
East Providence,	Rev. R. H. Paine,	Watchemoket.
Exeter, · ·	Willet H Arnold, ·	Exeter.
Foster, ·	George S. Tillinghast, ·	Foster Centre.
Glocester, ·	Rev. John M. Purkis.	Chepachet.
Hopkinton,	Rev. S. S. Griswold, ·	Hopkinton.
Jamestown, ·	Elijah Anthony, ·	Jamestown.
Johnston, ·	William A. Phillips,	Olneyville.
Lincoln. ·	Rev. James H. Lyon, ·	Central Falls.
Little Compton,	Benjamin F. Wilbor, Jr.,	Little Compton.
Middletown, ·	John Gould, · ·	Newport.
New Shoreham, ·	Giles H. Peabody, · ·	New Shoreham.
North Kingstown, ·	A. B. Chadsey, · ·	Wickford.
North Providence, ·	Marcus M. Cowing, ·	Providence.
North Smithfield, ·	Rev. Stephen Phillips, ·	Woonsocket.
Pawtucket,	Andrew Jencks, · ·	Pawtucket.
Portsmouth. ·	George Manchester,	Newport.
Richmond,	Rev. G. Tillinghast, ·	Wyoming.
Scituate, ·	Rev. J. M. Brewster, ·	North Scituate.
South Kingstown,	N. C. Peckham, Jr., ·	Wakefield.
Smithfield, ·	Hon. Samuel Farnum, ·	Georginville.
Tiverton, ·	John F. Chase, · ·	Fall River, Mass.
Warwick, ·	John F. Brown, ·	Natick.
Warren. · ·	Rev. S. K. Dexter, ·	Warren.
Westerly, ·	Rev. H. M. Eaton, · ·	Westerly.
West Greenwich, ·	Charles F. Carpenter, ·	Summit.
Woonsocket, ·	Rev. C. J. White, ·	Woonsocket.

* In nineteen towns the salaries of Superintendents are fixed. Maximum salary (Providence), $2,500; minimum salary, (Barrington), $25; Newport pays $2,000; Woonsocket, $500; Bristol, $400. One town pays $3 per day and expenses; one town $3 per day; one town $2.50 per day; one town has no fixed salary; two towns no salary; ten towns compensation not reported.

INDEX

To History of R. I. Institute of Instruction.

‒‒ ‒‒‒ ‒ ‒‒‒‒ ‒‒‒‒